Francie's Fortune

Kita Murdock

BLUE MUSTANG
P R E S S

Blue Mustang Press
Boston, Massachusetts

First printing

ISBN 978-1-935199-09-0
PUBLISHED BY BLUE MUSTANG PRESS
www.BlueMustangPress.com
Boston, Massachusetts

Printed in the United States of America

For Evie, Lucy and Noni

Chapter 1

Francie lay on her bed, staring at the ceiling and ignoring her mother's knocks on the door. Just a few hours before, she had walked home from school, arm in arm with her best friend Jenny, talking eagerly about their summer plans. They were both going to camp on Tuesdays and Thursdays and planned on spending the rest of the summer in Jenny's pool, as they had every summer that Francie could remember. Francie spent so much time at Jenny's that Jenny's mother often joked that she couldn't tell them apart, even though Jenny was dark with short, shiny, black hair and Francie was pale with frizzy, brown hair that drove her own mother crazy. When they got to Francie's house, they gave each other a quick hug.

"Come over after your snack!" Jenny called as Francie skipped up her front steps.

"Of course!" Francie yelled back, waving with one hand as she opened the door.

That's when everything changed.

Inside her house, Francie found her mother sitting at the table, drumming her fingers nervously, with a plate of homemade cookies on the table in front of her. Francie looked at the cookies and then back at her mother. Her mom was not a baking cookies kind of mom. Aside from half-empty take-out food boxes and the yogurt Francie usually ate after school, their refrigerator was generally empty. It occurred to Francie that the last time her mother had baked cookies was two years ago—the day she announced that Francie's father had moved out.

"What's going on?" Francie asked.

Her mother ignored the question. "How was school?" she asked, pushing the cookies toward Francie.

"Fine." She sat down, waiting for bad news.

"So, I have some good news," her mother said.

"Really?" Francie raised an eyebrow.

"I got a job." Her mother had been out of work for almost six months now, after the soap opera she had worked on for years was cancelled. After all of her auditions this year, a job was great news, but Francie still felt uneasy.

"That's great, Mom."

"Yeah, yeah, it's really great." She began tapping her hot pink fingernails on the table again.

"So what show is it?"

"Well, that's the thing, Francie. It's actually a movie." Her fingers moved from the table to a strand of platinum blonde hair that she twirled back and forth. "It's a great opportunity for me, but the thing is, it's not a permanent job. It's just for the summer. And, well, the other thing is, I have to be on location for the job." Her mother took a deep breath and put both of her hands flat on the table. "Francie, I have to go to New York for the summer and I can't bring you with me."

"So I have to stay with Dad?" Francie tried to imagine that. Her father only lived a few blocks away but she rarely saw him and had only stayed at his house a few times since her parents had separated two years ago, when Francie was eight years old.

"Not exactly. He's really busy this summer with work, Sweetie."

"Am I staying with Jenny?" Immediately Francie felt better. Staying all summer with her best friend would be like a three-month-long sleepover. She took a bite of one of the cookies.

"Francie, you're going to stay with my mother in Colorado. Your grandmother." Francie felt the dry cookie lodge in her throat. She tried to recall any information she could about her grandmother. It was strange her mother had even said the word "grandmother." She had always referred to her by her first name, Sylvie, in the rare occasions that she talked about her or about her childhood.

Francie knew that her mother had run away at eighteen to work as an actress in Los Angeles. After barely scraping by for several years, she finally landed a role as a receptionist on a popular soap opera. She met Francie's father, a successful Hollywood producer, at a party soon after that. They moved to Studio City and their current house, a medium-sized ranch house on a palm tree-lined street, when Francie was born. As far as Francie knew, her mother had only returned once, when Francie was two years old. Francie had heard her mother talking to a friend about how she had planned on staying for a week, but left after a couple of days.

"That place is so backwards. I don't think you could walk two feet in high heels without twisting your ankle in a pot hole, not that there's anywhere to go in high heels around there," her mother had complained to her friend Bev.

"I can't even begin to imagine you there, Justine," Bev had replied.

"Why do you think I got out of there as quick as a cat? Well, at least as quick as a cat wearing high heels." They both laughed.

Francie's grandmother had never come to Los Angeles, claiming that big cities made her nervous. At least that was the reason Francie's mother gave to her, rolling her eyes as she said it. If Francie hadn't received birthday cards from her grandmother every year, she might have forgotten she existed at all.

"I am going by myself to stay with Sylvie?" It felt strange to even say her name out loud.

"Yes. I think you should probably call her Grandmother. Or Grandma. Hmm, we'll have to ask her. Oh Francie, it'll be great. She lives in a small town in the mountains and there will be so much fun stuff to do. I think it'll be really good for you. I really do." Her mother flashed Francie an unconvincing smile. Francie glared at her.

"Be a good sport about it, okay Francie?" She picked up a cookie, took a bite, and then immediately spat it out in her napkin. "Ugh, these are awful! What do you say we take Jenny with us to go get some ice cream instead?" Her mother stood up.

"I don't even know her," Francie replied, not moving.

Her mother sighed and sat back down.

"She wrote me a letter recently, Francie, saying the same thing. That she doesn't even know you. She wants to know you. For Heaven's sake, she hasn't seen you in eight years. When I suggested this to her, she was, well, she was really excited about it."

Francie blinked to hold back tears.

"It's not my fault we haven't seen her in that long! You hate her and you hate where she lives and now you're sending me away to stay in some awful place in the middle of nowhere!"

Francie's mother's face flushed red. "Francie, that's not true."

"How long would I be gone for?"

"Just for the summer…"

"The whole summer!"

"Francie…"

At that, Francie had had enough. She stood up, knocking her chair over in the process, and ran to her room, slamming the door behind her.

An hour later, she still hadn't moved. She had listened as Jenny knocked at the front door and as her mother told her that she wasn't sure she'd be up for playing this afternoon. She had listened to her mother on the phone with her father, explaining how Francie wasn't very happy with the arrangement. Now she could hear Jenny and her brother splashing in their pool next door. She closed her eyes and tried not to think of all she would be missing this summer.

Chapter 2

The Denver Airport was a sea of people, but Francie spotted her grandmother right away. When she had asked her mother on the plane what Sylvie looked like, her mother had laughed.

"She looks like she's straight out of central casting. Just look for an old mountain woman, Francie."

Francie hadn't understood what that meant, but when she saw the woman in a faded brown dress with hiking boots and a gray braid to her knees, she knew it had to be Sylvie. Her skin was nut-brown from the sun and lined with wrinkles.

"Sylv—Mom!" her mother called, dragging Francie over to her. The old woman's face creased into a shy smile, exposing a chipped front tooth. Francie stepped backward toward her mother. Her mother stepped around Francie to give her grandmother an awkward hug. Francie thought to herself that they couldn't possibly look more different. Her mother, in her spiky heels, stood at least four inches above her grandmother. As usual, she was dressed in bright colors, with perfectly manicured nails, frosted pink lipstick and a bleached white smile. People stared at her, either because they recognized her as a receptionist at the hospital on a popular television show, or because they felt like they should recognize her somehow. Right now they were probably staring because they couldn't imagine why she would be hugging a woman who looked like she hadn't bought a new dress or had a haircut in years.

"Francie, this is your grandmother," her mother was saying, pulling her toward the old woman. She could tell her mom was nervous by the strained smile on her face. Francie leaned forward to give her grandmother a passable hug under her mom's stare. She was surprised that instead of smelling dirty, her grandmother smelled of pine needles and beeswax. When she stepped back, she noticed a bright gold locket hanging from her grandmother's neck.

"It's good to see you again," her grandmother said quietly.

"You too…Sylvie…I mean, Grandma." The words felt strange in her mouth.

"You can call me Sylvie if you like," she replied. Francie nodded.

Francie's mom chattered on the drive from the airport, telling Sylvie about the new movie and how happy she was that now they'd be able to afford to stay in their house in Studio City, and then about the various movie stars she would be working with and the fabulous apartment she had rented for the summer. She would be leaving the next morning, flying out of Denver to New York, and she seemed to have decided to make up for eight years of conversation in one car ride. Sylvie nodded from time to time, but was otherwise quiet. Francie sat in the back of the beat-up Volvo, looking out the window as the vast plains turned into steep cliffs. Her ears kept popping as the car climbed higher and higher up the road and into the mountains.

After a while, Francie fell asleep. She had spent the night before at a sleepover at Jenny's house and had hardly slept at all. As she slept in the car, she dreamed that she was a bird, flying in the air back to her house in Studio City. She had landed on a tree above Jenny's pool when a bump in the road jolted her awake. She felt her neck and rubbed the blue beaded necklace that Jenny tearfully gave her when she told her she'd be leaving for the summer. The bumps continued for another ten minutes, as the car climbed further into the mountains on a dirt road. When they came around a sharp turn, they could see Fortune, the small town in the valley, if you could even call it a town, that Sylvie called home, and that Francie would apparently call home for the next few months. It was nothing more than a few tired looking buildings surrounded by endless evergreen trees.

They continued past the town for another few minutes. When they came to a mailbox nearly covered with vines of purple flowers, Sylvie turned off the road down a short, pitted driveway and stopped in front of a wooden shack. The shack had once been brightly painted in blues and yellows, but years of sun had faded the paint. The windows of a greenhouse next to the shack reflected the late afternoon sunlight. Beyond the buildings, Francie could see nothing but tall, shadowy evergreen trees. Was her mother really leaving her here, in the middle of the wilderness, with a woman she barely knew? She briefly considered clinging onto the car seat and refusing to get out until they turned the car around and headed back to the airport. A few years ago she might have tried it but, at age ten, she knew it wouldn't result in anything more than embarrassment.

"Here we are," Sylvie said, turning off the car. She didn't look at Francie's mother, who had caught her breath mid-sentence.

"I forgot how small it is!" Francie's mother exclaimed in the same overly cheerful voice she had taken on ever since introducing the idea of Francie's summer plans.

When they entered tiny house, Francie was surprised to see that it was made up of only two rooms, if you counted the bathroom as a room…and if you counted the bathroom as a bathroom, given that it lacked a key element—the toilet. Sylvie pointed to a small dresser to the left of the door where Francie could put her belongings for the summer. Francie placed her backpack, full of her favorite books, on the dresser while her mother began unpacking her clothes out of her suitcase. She looked openly concerned for the first time since she had told Francie that she'd be living with her grandmother for the summer. Sylvie walked to the back of the room, where there was a small refrigerator, stove and sink, and then rows of shelves full of jars, in a variety of colors and sizes. Dried leaves hung from the ceiling tied with colorful yarn and Francie could smell a potpourri of herbs. The aroma helped soothe the churning in her stomach.

To the right of the kitchen area, Francie noticed a large bookshelf, jammed full of books on herbs and wildflowers. Next to that, patchwork quilts covered a bed and cot. Sylvie explained that Francie's mother would sleep in the cot for the night and Francie would sleep on some quilts on the floor. After that, the cot would be Francie's for the summer. There was a small wooden table with three chairs in front of the window in the other corner of the house and a round, frayed, woven rug on the floor. Potted flowers and plants nearly covered the windows. Behind the table, a door led into the bathroom, or the small shower room to be more precise. As Sylvie described how she had "an outhouse" out back, just a few steps outside, Francie found herself fighting back tears once again. Her mother stopped her nervous chatter for a moment and patted Francie on the arm, an acknowledgement of how terrible the situation actually was.

Once the quick tour was over, Sylvie pulled a large cast iron pot out of the refrigerator and placed it on the stove. Soon the pot was bubbling and Francie realized that she was hungry. Sylvie served them warm bean stew in homemade ceramic bowls at the small table. Francie surprised herself and her mother by finishing her bowl and then having another. Usually her mom could hardly get her to eat.

After dinner, her grandmother sat with Francie's mother while Francie opened up her backpack and pulled out *Charlie and the Chocolate Factory*. She wanted to forget that she was stuck in a small cabin with an old lady she didn't know for the next few months. Instead she tried to imagine herself as Charlie for the rest of the evening, exploring a world full of magical surprises with his grandfather. But even her favorite book couldn't serve as a distraction from her situation. The words kept blurring as her eyes filled with tears.

Before bed, her mother walked out back with her to the outhouse. Francie focused on the flashlight's trail of light and tried not to look around otherwise. If she hadn't been so scared, she might have laughed at the image of her mother tiptoeing around pine cones in the dark in her lavender silk nightgown. Instead, she wondered how she would make this walk at night by herself for the rest of the summer. They didn't speak until she got inside and her mother kissed her goodnight.

"I love you," her mother whispered and then gave her a quick, tight hug.

Francie didn't sleep well that night. She kept waking up, listening to her mother and grandmother snoring (in that aspect at least, they were similar). She also could hear all sorts of unfamiliar noises— squeaks and rustling and once a shrieking sound outside that sent shivers up her spine.

Just after she finally fell into a deeper sleep, her mother woke her up with a kiss on the cheek to tell her that the taxi was here and she was leaving. Groggy with sleep, Francie was confused where she was or what exactly was happening. By the time she came to her senses, her mother was gone, leaving nothing but a frosted pink lipstick smudge on Francie's cheek.

Chapter 3

As her eyes adjusted to the dim light, Francie realized Sylvie was already out of her bed, making tea at the stove. She contemplated pretending that she was still asleep, but Sylvie turned to her and smiled, asking her how she had slept.

"Okay, thanks," she answered, pushing aside the quilt and standing up. "But, um, I have to go to the bathroom again."

Sylvie pointed to the door and said, "The sun's starting to come up so you shouldn't need a flashlight. Oh, and remember to add a scoop of sawdust to the toilet when you're done."

"Sawdust?"

"It's a composting toilet. No water."

Francie sighed. She hadn't even noticed in the dark. She put on her flip flops, opened the door and was surprised by the cold.

"It'll warm up later in the day," Sylvie told her as she stepped back inside to grab a sweatshirt from her small dresser.

Outside, the sky was still gray to the west, but to the east she could see the glimmer of the sun. The birds were awake for the morning and, instead of the noise of traffic that Francie usually heard at home, she listened to their chirps and tweets filling the air. She tried not to think about what might have caused the shrieking sound she had heard at night. She walked to the back to the small, wooden building Sylvie had pointed out yesterday, wishing her mother was still leading the way. The door opened with a creak and Francie took a deep breath. There were crescent moon-shaped holes for light cut in the wood at the top of the outhouse, but with the door closed behind her, it would be almost pitch black. She took a careful look with the door open and saw what she was glad she hadn't noticed the night before—six spiders on the wall. Did she really have to go? She decided that not only did she have to go, but that she clearly couldn't hold it all summer. She went as quickly as she could, adding a scoop of sawdust to the toilet when she was finished. She imagined her first postcard to Jenny:

Life is great in Fortune. I get to pee outside with the spiders. XO, Francie

When she walked back to the house, the sun already appeared a bit higher in the sky. Inside, Sylvie placed two mugs of mint tea with honey and toast with wild raspberry jam on the table. She told Francie that she had picked the raspberries just two days ago and that perhaps they could go together to pick some more. They sipped their tea. The cabin seemed unnaturally quiet without her mother filling it up with talk.

"I thought maybe I'd give you a tour of Fortune this morning. What do you think?"

Francie shrugged, thinking that would probably take about two minutes.

"Until then, I have to pick some herbs to bring to Augustus's store. Do you want to help me?"

"Okay."

Francie's grandmother led Francie outside to the greenhouse next to the house. When they walked inside, Francie was amazed at the number of flowers and plants growing everywhere she looked. They hung from the ceiling, crawled up stakes against the windows and stood in countless rows on the ground. Sylvie handed her gloves and pointed out which herbs to pick. They started with rosemary. Francie recognized the pine-like scent and wondered if Sylvie had been picking rosemary in the greenhouse before picking her up at the airport the day before. They moved on to pick basil, thyme and then a variety of herbs that Francie had never heard of before. After they had collected an armful each, they went inside to rinse them off and sort them into bags.

Sylvie then explained that they would be bringing both fresh and dried herbs to the store. After laying the fresh herbs on the table, she pulled down several dried plants that were hanging from the ceiling.

"People drive from all over to buy my herbs and tinctures and teas made from these herbs," she said. She sounded shy but proud at the same time. Francie helped her unwind the string from the herbs and mix them into bags as Sylvie explained the benefits of comfrey, feverfew and valerian, all of which she had grown in her garden or greenhouse.

As they had bagged and labeled the herbs, Francie looked up and noticed four squirrels peering in at them from the window. She jumped in her seat and dropped the herbs back on the table.

"Is that normal?" Francie asked, pointing to the window. She turned to Sylvie, who was busy filling a backpack with herbs and didn't seem to hear her.

"Ready to go?" Sylvie asked.

Francie glanced back at the window, but the squirrels were gone.

It was a twenty-minute walk into town and as they walked, Francie noticed how clean the air felt in her lungs. She took a deep breath. *Well, at least there's one thing about Fortune*, she thought, *no smog.* But then she noticed that she was short of breath and struggling to keep up with Sylvie, which made no sense. Sylvie explained that it takes time to adjust to the high altitude and that Francie would be running around like normal in no time.

The entire town of Fortune consisted of seven buildings. The town hall didn't look much bigger than Sylvie's house and could have easily been mistaken for a rundown shack except for the white painted sign reading "Fortune Town Hall" which was hanging slightly off-kilter. Next to the town hall was an even smaller building, with a taped-over broken window. The sign above the door read "Fortune Gold Mining Museum" in faded yellow paint. Under it was what looked like a painting of a donkey and a man holding a pan. Francie's grandmother explained that the town of Fortune was started when a small group of men came through, prospecting for gold in the late 1850s. They found enough in the river to encourage them to stay for a few months and for others to hear about it and come searching there as well. But the supply was quickly depleted and, when larger amounts of gold were discovered at Pike's Peak, most of the men moved on. Sylvie's great-grandfather stayed. He wrote to his wife and told her that he couldn't imagine living anywhere else. He would come back to Chicago to get her and the kids and to load up the wagons. He couldn't wait to show her their new home. Sylvie's family had lived there ever since.

"That is," she said, "until your mother and her father left. Now there's just me."

Francie thought about that. Her mother had never talked about her father except to say that he had left when she was six years old and she hadn't seen him since. A hundred questions about her mother and her family ran through Francie's head, but Sylvie pointed to the coffee shop and began talking about local tourists so Francie understood that was the end of the subject for now.

At the Bald Mountain Coffee Shoppe, a young couple wearing Patagonia fleece jackets and scruffy hiking boots sat holding steaming mugs on the front porch. Sylvie explained that they were likely here for hiking or rock climbing in the nearby mountains. Joe's Pizza was across the street, with a "Closed" sign hanging on the door and a sign flashing "BE" in the window. The "ER" was unlit. Next to that was Cold Creek Apparel & Outdoor Goods, the Crystal and Gem Store, and then, at the end of the street, with no sign out front, the food co-op.

As they walked in the food co-op, it struck Francie that this little dingy strip was it. This was where she would be all summer long. She thought of her house in Studio City, where she could walk to at least twenty restaurants, endless shops and both a Giant and a Von's grocery store. She felt a sharp pang of homesickness as she pictured herself and Jenny sitting in front of the Baskin Robbins, trading bites of ice cream. They always tried to get the most bizarre combination—one scoop of mint chocolate chip with a scoop of cotton candy or birthday cake swirl with rocky road. She wondered if you could even get ice cream in Fortune.

Her question answered as soon as they walked in the co-op door. A large metal bin to the right read "Sally's Homemade Ice Cream. All Natural. Vanilla, Chocolate, Strawberry." Obviously she wouldn't be eating cotton candy ice cream this summer.

Jenny – I'm going to miss our ice cream afternoons more than I even thought. Guess how many flavors they have in Fortune? Give up? Three. XO, Francie

The co-op didn't look anything like the grocery stores Francie knew from home. It looked more like a combination of a farmer's market and someone's attic. There were bins and boxes everywhere, full of local fruit and vegetables, flour, oats or other items that were unrecognizable to her.

Francie noticed a wooden sign that read "Post Office" in the corner, with dusty looking envelopes and boxes on a shelf on the wall. She walked over to a rack of postcards and spun it around. She picked out one that read "Find your fortune in Fortune!" in sprawling white letters with a picture of the Fortune Gold Mining Museum underneath and then one of a woman in bell bottoms standing in a field of purple wildflowers. Francie guessed that the postcards had been sitting there at the co-op ever since bell bottoms were in style.

"Can I get these to send to my friend Jenny?" she asked Sylvie.

Sylvie looked at the postcards she had selected and smiled.

"Of course. Get as many as you need. Then tomorrow I can start to give you an allowance for helping me around the house and in the garden. You can use the money to buy whatever you would like in here."

"That sounds good," Francie said and pulled out a couple more postcards. She had never had a real allowance before. Her mother gave her money when she needed it to go to the movies or get ice cream, but she liked the idea of having money that was truly her own. Of course, there was nothing much to buy with it in Fortune but postcards and plain ice cream.

As she walked up to the counter, Francie noticed that nature photographs in black frames covered the walls of the co-op. Most were of flowers or evergreens. One was a landscape of a snow-capped mountain.

"Is that Bald Mountain? Like the coffee shop?" Francie asked, pointing to the picture.

Sylvie nodded. "That's the one," she replied.

The store was empty aside from an old man in a baseball cap and flannel at the counter. He had a thick white moustache and shaggy gray hair sticking out from under his hat. A purple scar ran from the corner of his eye down the middle of his left cheek. Sylvie walked up to him and placed her backpack on the counter.

"Augustus," she said.

"Sylvie," he replied. Apparently this was their way of greeting. He looked curiously at Francie.

"This is my…granddaughter. Francie. She is staying with me this summer."

Augustus raised his eyebrows. "Nice to meet you," he said after a second, smiling and extending his hand over the counter.

"You too," Francie replied, placing the postcards down and shaking his warm, dry hand.

She watched as Sylvie sorted through the bags of herbs, explaining each one to Augustus. He nodded silently, inspecting each bag. At one point, he put a bag down and his hand brushed against Sylvie's on the counter. He jumped as if he'd been bitten by a snake. Both he and Sylvie blushed red. He quickly paid her, subtracting the cost of the postcards. Francie followed as Sylvie hurried out of the store.

"He thinks I'm a witch," she said harshly to Francie as they walked back up the road.

Francie was so taken aback that she stumbled over a stone in the road and dropped her postcards on the ground. As she bent down to pick them up, she found herself wondering if Sylvie was in fact a witch. She obviously wasn't a fairy tale witch with a black hat and cape, but didn't those witches usually disguise themselves as old women anyway? She thought about how Sylvie lived alone in a cabin, surrounded by dark woods. But Augustus lived in Fortune too, he could hardly find that unusual. She looked at Sylvie, who had bent down to help Francie. Sylvie handed Francie a postcard with a shy smile.

"Sorry, I didn't mean to scare you," she said. Then, noticing something next to the road, she walked over and asked Francie to follow. She pointed out a patch of dandelions to Francie and bent over to pick some of the leaves.

"Have you seen these before?"

"Sure, they're dandelions. Weeds, right?" Francie could picture the gardeners who came to her house every week spraying the dandelions to keep the lawn looking perfectly green.

"Some people see these as just weeds," Sylvie replied, "and

certainly they can take over a garden. But they are wonderful either sautéed or steamed. We'll have some for dinner tonight with garlic and chopped onions. You can see if you like them."

Francie leaned over to help pick more dandelion greens. Sylvie's voice was so warm and cheerful that Francie decided to push any thoughts of witches from her mind.

Chapter 4

When they got back to the house, Sylvie told Francie that they would need to do some cleaning in the house and in the greenhouse. She handed Francie a broom, which brought Francie's mind back to the witch comment. Before Francie could begin sweeping, Sylvie changed her mind.

"You know what? It's your first day here and it's beautiful out. We'll work tomorrow. Today let's hike down to the creek," Sylvie said, and immediately began busying herself with preparing for their walk.

Francie had never done any hiking before, but her mom had predicted that she would be doing some this summer and had bought her new hiking boots. Another wave of homesickness washed over Francie as she remembered going shopping for the boots with her mom. She hadn't talked to her on the way to the store, angry that they would be buying boots for a summer in Fortune instead of clothes for camp in Studio City. But when she grudgingly tried the boots on, her mom hugged her, thanking her for being such a wonderful daughter and had told her that she was working for both of them and promised she would make up for this summer in the long run.

"You'll have so many stories to tell me at the end of the summer," her mom had encouraged as they both looked down at the sturdy brown hiking boots. Thinking of the dull main street she had just seen, Francie doubted this was true, but as she tied the laces of her boots, she missed her mom.

They headed out with the same backpack they had carried to the co-op that morning. This time it was full with two peanut butter and raspberry jelly sandwiches, a bag of cherries, and a jug of water. Francie and Sylvie were both quiet as they walked, but the singing birds in the trees kept the woods far from silent. Sylvie walked easily while Francie had to concentrate not to slip on roots and rocks on the narrow trail. After about an hour of hiking, Sylvie directed her to walk off the trail. They walked through a patch of tall, purple flowers with petals that looked like flames.

"They look like the flowers in the postcard," Francie noted. Sylvie told her they were shooting stars. Soon Francie could hear the rush of running water.

They walked down the mossy bank to Cold Creek. Francie could see the smooth, gray rocks at the bottom where the water pooled. Sylvie set the backpack down in the moss next to the creek and pulled off her hiking boots and socks. Francie gladly did the same, as she could already feel burning blisters on both of her heels. They dipped their feet into the creek and Francie pulled back in shock at the coldness of the water.

"The creek is aptly named. It's snow-melt," Sylvie told her. "About as cold as it can get!"

After a couple of seconds, it didn't feel as bad and Francie kept her feet soaking.

"Is there any gold left in the creek?" Francie asked, thinking of the Fortune Gold Mining Museum.

"Probably not," Sylvie laughed. "There wasn't even much when they started looking all those years ago."

They sat there with their feet in the water, eating their sandwiches. After a while, Francie noticed a surprising number of birds on the trees and flying above them.

"Wow, there are a lot of birds in these woods, huh?"

Sylvie stopped chewing for a moment. She seemed to pause, as if she weren't sure of something. Then she shook her head slightly and began pointing out the birds—the Williamson's Sapsucker, Yellow Warbler, Song Sparrow and American Goldfinch.

"We have hummingbirds at home," Francie told her. She had a feeder hanging from the orange tree in her yard and often sat on her bed, watching the bright green birds flitting by her window. Almost as if on queue, a gray hummingbird with pale yellow wings buzzed above them. Francie laughed out loud in delight. Sylvie shook her head again, as if trying to shake away a thought. The hummingbird darted away. They sat in silence again.

"I used to take your mother here," Sylvie said after a while. Francie tried to picture her mother as a young child, sitting by the creek with her feet in the water. When she pictured her mother's feet, she pictured them at the spa, where she often took Francie on weekends. Francie would get her nails painted with different colored flowers while her mother got a French Manicure.

"I can't imagine my mom hiking," she replied, laughing. She realized she couldn't picture her mom as a little girl either, or her grandmother as a young mother.

"She never was very fond of it. Or, really very fond of Fortune to tell you the truth." Sylvie looked down and sighed. "But she would still come down here with me." She looked up and turned to Francie. "You know, she was an actress even then. I remember one time we came down here and she acted out all of the kids she knew. She had them spot on too. She has some real talent."

Francie nodded. Her mom did have talent. She had heard it all of her life.

"Talent and looks, you've got 'em both, Baby," one of her mom's boyfriends had said once to her mother. He'd turned to Francie and asked if she agreed. Francie had nodded silently, feeling that he was reminding her that, unlike her mother, she had neither.

Once, when she was in kindergarten, she had left art class, and a painting that even then she knew to be unimpressive, to go to the bathroom. While washing her hands, she had looked at herself in the bathroom mirror and was struck with the thought that she was nothing more than two dots and a line. Two muddy brown eyes, a thin mouth, plain and boring, and a nose too small to count—all surrounded by a mess of dull colored hair. Everyone else in her class had something unique about the way they looked—freckles or long black braids, bright blue eyes or even a big, interesting nose. She had rushed home from school that day, crying. Her mother had asked her what was wrong, but when Francie had sobbed, "I am just two dots and a line," her mother just shook her head. "I'm sorry you're upset Francie, but sometimes I just have no idea what you're talking about," she replied. And of course she wouldn't.

Her mother never said it to her, but Francie sensed that she felt disappointed that her daughter wasn't more like her. She had even signed her up for a theater class once but Francie hated getting up in front of everyone and had spent the class slouched in her seat with her head down, hoping the teacher wouldn't call on her. Her mother didn't sign her up again.

After they finished their lunch, they sat by the creek for a while, listening to the flowing water and singing birds. Sylvie dipped her hand in the water and began swirling it around absentmindedly. Suddenly, to Francie's surprise, dozens of fish began leaping out of the water. They sparkled in the sunlight and almost seemed to dance as they jumped through the air.

"That's amazing!" Francie exclaimed. "I had no idea fish did that!" Sylvie pulled her hand out abruptly and the fish flopped back into the water. Francie reached in and began swirling her own hand around. She could feel the pulse of energy from the fish flowing through the water and into her hand. She swirled her hand faster and the fish began jumping into the air again, as if they were putting on a show.

28

"It's so beautiful!" she cried. She looked over at Sylvie, but Sylvie had pulled herself up and was looking as if she'd seen a ghost. "What's wrong?" Francie asked, shaking the water off her hand. "It's…it's my arthritis. I need to get home," Sylvie replied. She grabbed her backpack and began heading up the hill. Francie didn't know much about arthritis, but it struck her as odd that Sylvie was speeding home if she didn't feel well. Once again, Francie's breath came in loud pants as she tried to keep up with the old woman.

When they got back to the house, Sylvie spun toward Francie and stared at her for a minute, searching her face. Francie bit her lip, unable to understand what Sylvie wanted from her.

"I need to rest. I am going to take a nap for a little bit," Sylvie finally said.

"I'm not really tired," Francie replied, wondering if she expected her to take a nap as well. Somehow she felt that Sylvie wanted her as far away as possible at that moment, but she wasn't sure exactly where to go.

"Yes, of course. You play outside for a little bit." With that, Sylvie closed the door. Francie stared at the closed door in stunned silence. What had just happened? What had gone wrong?

Chapter 5

Francie walked to the end of the short dirt driveway and thought about walking into town. Her blisters were still burning her feet though and a walk didn't seem that appealing. In fact, she wasn't sure she could even keep her boots on for another minute. She sat down and pulled off her boots, inspecting the red welts on her feet and thinking about how the summer was going even worse than she had imagined.

She thought of another postcard for Jenny:

We walked down to the creek. The fish were beautiful, jumping out of the water and into the air. XO, Francie

She decided to leave out Sylvie's strange reaction. However, her postcard writing would have to wait until evening, as she wasn't about to go back into the house.

Francie was so intent on looking at her blisters and thinking about Jenny that she didn't even notice the boy standing in front of her until he kicked dirt at her, spraying it into her eyes. She jerked her head up, wiping her eyes, to find a boy about her age standing next to his bike in front of her. His hair was so blonde it looked almost white and he had more freckles than she'd ever seen on anyone before.

"What was that for?" she asked, wiping more dirt off her face.

"I've been standing here for about an hour and you didn't even look up."

"First of all, it couldn't have been an hour. I've only been here for a minute. And anyway, haven't you ever heard of just saying hello?"

He laughed and smiled a devilish smile.

"Want to go for a bike ride?"

"I don't have a bike here," she replied.

"We could walk to my house. It's just down the road. My sister has a bike you can use. Might be a little small for you."

"I hate biking," she answered, not wanting to admit that she didn't know how to ride.

"You *hate* biking?" He looked at her skeptically. "Alright then, do you want to go down the stream for a swim?"

"No!" she replied angrily.

"Do you hate swimming too?"

"No." She sighed, thinking of Jenny's pool.

"Okaaay, well, you sure are fun." He shook his head and hopped onto his bike. Suddenly Francie realized that even if he had just kicked dirt in her face, she didn't want him to leave her sitting here at the end of the driveway in the middle of nowhere with nothing to do.

"Wait. I mean, what's your name?"

"Ronan," he responded, taking his foot off the pedal.

"I'm Francie."

"Do you live with Sylvie now or something?" he asked, gesturing toward the cabin.

"How do you know Sylvie?"

Ronan laughed. "There are about two hundred people living around here. Everyone knows everyone."

"Well, I don't really live with her. I mean, I'm just here for the summer. Do you live near here?"

"Yup, just up the road."

They looked at each other for a second.

"Okay, see you around," Ronan said.

"Wait! I mean, I don't really hate biking. I just…I don't know how to bike. I've never even tried." Ronan's eyes widened in surprise. "But I'd still like to hang out. My grandmother is sleeping and I'm just sitting here with nothing to do."

"How old are you?"

"Ten."

"Hey, me too. Wait, you're ten and you don't know how to bike? My little sister is five and a half and she already…"

"Look, forget it," Francie interrupted, standing up.

"Never mind," Ronan said. "You can't stay here all summer without biking. I'll teach you how to bike." He jumped off his bike and patted the seat. Francie looked back at the house and the closed door. Then she grabbed the handlebars and swung her leg over the bike.

"Don't you want to put shoes on first?" Ronan asked. She pointed at her blisters and shook her head.

"Okay, suit yourself," he replied. "Now you know how to pedal, right?" Francie nodded, her heart pounding.

"So I'm going to give you a little push and you just keep pedaling," Ronan said, gripping onto the seat from behind.

"How is that going to teach me?" Francie asked, but he'd already pushed and a minute later she was sprawled out on the dirt road, with dirt and pebbles ground into her knees and elbows.

"You really don't know how to ride, huh?"

Francie brushed herself off and looked at the bike.

"I'll give it another try." This time she actually biked a little further and then managed to slam her feet onto the ground before falling off the bike. The right pedal smacked into her shin and she winced in pain. Ronan jogged to keep up.

"You did pretty good," Ronan encouraged, sounding somewhat doubtful. Francie decided to try again and slowly, stopping and slamming her feet down every minute, she made her way down the road, with Ronan alongside her. By the time they got to Ronan's house, along with having swollen blisters on her feet, her front toe was bleeding, shins were bruised, and elbows and knees were covered in scrapes.

"Who the heck are you?" a girl asked from the front stoop of a house that looked almost identical to Francie's grandmother's, except that it had a chicken coop to the right of it instead of a greenhouse. The chickens clucked noisily as they arrived.

"Francie," she replied, handing the bike over to Ronan, who left it on its side in the grass. The girl, who Francie assumed was Ronan's sister, had the same white-blonde hair and almost as many freckles.

"You look kinda beat up."

"Yeah, I know," Francie sighed.

"Yeah, but you just learned how to ride a bike! I mean, you're close at least. A couple more tries," Ronan encouraged.

Ronan's mother called from inside the house.

"Ronan! Where you been? I need you to watch Rosie while I run to the store!" The door opened and a fat woman in jeans and a tank top stepped out. Ronan was skin and bones, but Francie could see where the hair and freckles came from.

"Who are you?" she asked Francie, in a tone not unlike the one her daughter had just used.

"Francie," she replied again.

Ronan's mother looked her over. "Well, Francie, what happened to you?"

Francie looked down at her knees. "Ronan taught me to ride a bike," she replied.

"Looks like he taught you how to fall is more like it!" Ronan's mom disappeared into the house and came back with a warm, damp washcloth. Francie sat on the stoop and pressed the washcloth against her bleeding toe.

"You gonna be alright?" Ronan's mom asked, looking at Francie's bruised shins.

34

"I'm fine," Francie replied, smiling. "Thank you for the washcloth."

"Where'd you come from?" Ronan's mother asked.

"Well, I came from Los Angeles but I'm staying with my grandma this summer."

Ronan's mom let out a hoot of a laugh. "You live in Los Angeles? Tell me something, how are you adjusting to life out here in the sticks?" She laughed again. Before Francie could answer, she walked out the door and into the pick-up truck parked out front.

"Back in a minute," she called from the driver's seat and the truck pulled away.

Ronan went inside and came back a minute later with popsicles for himself, Francie and Rosie.

"So you don't have cotton candy ice cream, but you do have popsicles," Francie mused.

"Huh?" Rosie looked up at her.

"Never mind," she replied, sitting on the stoop licking her cherry popsicle.

"Where do fish take a tub?" Ronan asked.

"What?" Francie asked, trying to figure out what he was talking about.

"In the bass tub," Rosie replied, rolling her eyes. "That's a bad one Ronan. Plus I've heard it a million billion times."

"I have one," Francie said, grinning. "What kind of dance do you do on a trampoline?"

"A jumping dance?" Rosie asked.

"Hip hop," Francie replied.

"You guys are terrible," Rosie said, but she laughed. For the next hour, they sat there on the stoop in the sun, licking their popsicles (three each, even though Rosie told Ronan that "Mom will kill you!") and telling jokes. Francie almost forgot that she was homesick and stuck in a dingy town with a grandmother who suddenly wanted nothing to do with her.

35

Chapter 6

Y ou lazy bums are still sitting out here!" Ronan's mom exclaimed when she returned in the truck. "Don't you kids have chores to do?"

"I should be getting back," Francie said, standing up. She dreaded going back to Sylvie's, but she didn't want to be around when Ronan's mom discovered the empty popsicle box either. "Thanks for the bike lesson, Ronan."

He gave her a crooked smile. "Any time."

Francie walked back up the road, her throbbing bare feet dragging in the dirt, and thought about how it had turned out to be a pleasant afternoon after all. She was glad she hadn't already written Jenny a postcard. She was looking forward to including that she had learned how to ride a bike.

The walk seemed longer on the way home. Francie thought about it and decided that walking probably took longer than biking, even if she had crashed every few minutes on the bike. Still, after a while she began to worry. The road looked exactly as it had by Ronan's house—a pothole-filled dirt road, with scrubby grass to either side and endless evergreen trees—but Ronan's house was no longer visible and neither was Sylvie's. She had been so focused on riding the bike on the way down that she hadn't noticed whether or not she had taken any turns. She racked her brain, trying to remember, and considered that perhaps she had walked right by Sylvie's house. The only indication of her driveway was a mailbox that was nearly covered with vines and Francie hadn't been paying close attention.

She turned, facing the way she had come, and asked herself out loud, "Okay, should I turn around or not?"

As if in answer, something made a noise behind her. Francie turned around and caught her breath. There, in the middle of the road, a large mountain lion stood staring at her. The lion didn't move, but just looked at her with pale yellow eyes. A scar ran down its face, from the tip of its nose to the corner of its eye.

For a second, Francie didn't move either. She felt frozen, as if an electric current held her in place. Then the lion opened its mouth slightly and Francie caught a glimpse of its long, yellow teeth. Francie's vision blurred and the lion and the road seemed to sway in front of her. Then she came to her senses and turned and ran as fast as she could go. She didn't stop until her breath was so ragged that she thought she might collapse. When she finally looked back, she saw no sign of the mountain lion and began to walk, gasping for air.

Soon, she came across her hiking boots, tossed on the side of the road before Sylvie's driveway and sighed with relief. Even a grumpy grandmother didn't seem like much of a threat compared to a lion.

When she walked toward the house, she could see Sylvie sitting at the table by the window. Sylvie looked at Francie when she walked in and drew in a deep breath.

"Francie!" she gasped, "What on earth happened to you? You're covered in blood!"

Francie looked down and imagined how she might look to Sylvie—scrapes and cuts everywhere and dark red popsicle juice all over her shirt and face.

"Well, most of this isn't blood. It's mostly popsicle juice. And some cuts from learning to bike. But…I almost got eaten by a lion." Her voice quivered.

"What do you mean?"

"Well, there was a lion in the road when I was coming back."

"What did you do?" Sylvie asked, searching her face.

"I ran of course!"

"Oh, Francie," she stood up and gave her a hug. "I am glad you are mostly covered in popsicle juice. You know, I'm sure you were scared. I should have told you that we have mountain lions around here. If that happens again, you really should never run from a mountain lion. They can run much faster than you can. And if you start running, you can trigger the mountain lion to chase after you." Francie looked at Sylvie. She sounded calm, even as she warned Francie what to do.

"What should I have done?" Francie asked.

"You could have talked to her and then backed away. Slowly. You would've been fine."

"Well," she replied angrily, "fortunately I was fine. But it could have killed me."

Sylvie looked at her again. "No, she wouldn't have done that," she said, her voice thoughtful. "But never mind that now. Let's get you cleaned up. So how did you manage to get so much popsicle juice all over you?"

As Francie explained about eating popsicles on Ronan's porch and about learning to ride a bike, she started to feel better. Despite the mountain lion and Sylvie's strange behavior by the creek, she had enjoyed her afternoon.

When Francie's mother called that night, she had a different response to Francie's story. She shrieked in her ear and then told her over and over again that she loved her and even asked if she should come get her. Francie had been wanting to hear those words, but when her mother offered, Francie knew she didn't want her to accept. She told her that she was alright and she would give Fortune more of a chance. Her mother sounded relieved and then asked to

39

speak to Sylvie. Francie listened as Sylvie reassured her over and over that Francie was safe and that she promised nothing would happen to her.

Before she went to bed, Francie pulled out a postcard with a picture of a mountain creek on the front. There was no description of the picture on the back of the postcard, but Francie imagined it must be Cold Creek. She wrote the postcard to Jenny that she had been imagining all day:

Dear Jenny - I can't believe it's only been one day! I feel like I've been gone for weeks already. Today I saw lots of spiders and went on a hike and saw flying fish and learned to ride a bike AND I saw a mountain lion!!! I MISS YOU! XO, Francie

\- \- \-

That night, despite the altitude and Sylvie's snoring, Francie collapsed into bed and slept through the night. She dreamed again that she was a bird, flying home to Studio City. This time, when she landed on a tree by Jenny's pool, she looked in the pool and saw that instead of Jenny, there was a mountain lion paddling around in the water and the water was full of shimmering fish. She woke up with a start, but by then the sun was already shining through the windows. It was morning.

Chapter 7

The next week passed rather uneventfully, at least compared to Francie's first day in Fortune. She spent her mornings helping Sylvie in the garden and learning about the different herbs, vegetables and flowers that she grew. With all of the weeding, planting, watering and picking that needed to be done, the garden provided endless work. But Francie found herself enjoying the smell of the plants and the feeling of the soft, dry dirt on her hands and warm sun on her back. Sylvie would point out certain weeds to Francie or talk to her about the purposes of the different herbs, but mostly they worked quietly. The garden itself was far from quiet though and Francie enjoyed the music of the birds and the bugs that chirped and hummed alongside her.

Sylvie never mentioned the incident at the creek or what it had meant. Francie still wondered if she had said or done something wrong, but if she had, Sylvie seemed to have forgiven her.

Francie spent most of her afternoons with Ronan, who usually biked up to Sylvie's and then they would ride into town on his bike with Francie on the seat and Ronan standing up and pedaling. Sometimes Rosie would let her borrow her bike, but once she discovered that Francie and Ronan would take off with both bikes, she complained that it wasn't fair. In a few days, Rosie would be going to her aunt's house for two weeks and Ronan told Francie that she could use the bike while Rosie was gone.

Sylvie gave Francie a small allowance and she spent most of it on ice cream in town. She and Ronan would ride his bike into town and then stop at the food co-op and order vanilla or chocolate cones. They'd sit on the stoop, licking the cones and talking about what to do for the rest of the day. Whenever Francie went to the counter, Augustus would ask her the same thing.

"How is your grandma doing, Francie?"

"She's fine."

"That's good. That's good to hear," he always responded.

\- \- \-

"Augustus seems friendly enough to me," Francie said to Ronan one afternoon.

"Sure, why wouldn't he be?" he asked.

She shrugged in reply.

Once, when Ronan and Francie were eating ice cream on the stoop, Francie complained that in Studio City they served much more fun flavors of ice cream—cotton candy and birthday cake and marshmallow swirl. Ronan had looked down at both of their vanilla cones and then smiled his crooked smile.

"We can do that here too."

Francie followed him inside as he picked out a bag full of gummy worms and another of chocolate chips. He asked Augustus if he had a plastic spoon and, after some rummaging through the drawers at the counter, Augustus found a dusty spoon for them. He cleaned it off with his shirt and handed it to Francie. Outside, Francie watched as Ronan dumped the ice cream from both of their cones out into the bag of gummy worms and then poured in the chocolate chips as well. After mixing them up, he used the spoon to scoop the half-melted ice cream back onto their cones. The ice cream poured down the side of Francie's cone, but she laughed and had to admit that it tasted just as good as any ice cream she had ever tried.

Jenny - We made gummy worm ice cream today. The one flavor they don't have at home. Miss you!
XO, Francie

When she wrote the postcard that night, she realized that two weeks had already passed.

Chapter 8

One afternoon, when both Francie and Ronan had run out of ice cream money, Ronan suggested again that they head down to the creek. Francie looked toward the house, as if Sylvie might come running out in objection somehow, but Sylvie was gardening behind the house and the door remained closed.

"It'd be fun. We could go swimming down there," Ronan said. It was an unusually hot day and Francie had to admit that sounded nice. She ran inside and changed out of flip flops and into her hiking boots, glad that her blisters had finally healed, and they headed down toward the creek.

The woods seemed quieter than they had when Francie hiked to the creek with Sylvie. She noticed that fewer birds flew around their heads and she only heard sporadic chirps up in the trees. But whenever Francie heard the crack of a stick or rustle of leaves near them, she jumped.

"I'm still thinking about that mountain lion," she explained to Ronan when he laughed as she let out a small shriek when a squirrel ran across the trail.

"My dad wants to shoot the mountain lion that keeps coming on our property. Keeps eating the chickens," Ronan replied.

"What would you do if we saw one right here?" Francie asked.

"I don't think we need to worry about it so much. It's really weird that you saw one in the afternoon. Usually they only come out at night. C'mon, let's get to the stream. Last one in gets eaten by a mountain lion!" Ronan began to run and Francie caught up with him, running until they reached the river bed.

Ronan seemed to toss off his shirt and sneakers and dive in without breaking stride, but Francie stopped to take off her hiking boots. When she jumped into the creek, the coldness of the water took her breath away. She quickly hopped out, gasping for air, unable to imagine that she had been sweating a minute ago. Ronan splashed her and then pulled himself up to the side of the bank. They sat there, kicking their feet in the water, much like Francie and Sylvie had.

"It's weird there aren't so many fish today," Francie commented, looking into the water.

"I hardly ever see fish in here," Ronan replied.

"Last time I was here there were tons of fish. It was cool too—they were jumping out of the water almost like they were dancing. It was beautiful."

"No way," said Ronan, shaking his head.

Francie was silent for a minute. She remembered how Sylvie had gotten upset about the fish for some reason, but Sylvie was up in the cabin and didn't even know Francie was by the creek.

Francie dipped her fingers into the water, swirling them around as she had that first time at the creek. Just as before, fish suddenly began leaping out of the water. Their silver gills shone in the sun and once again they appeared to be dancing in the air. The cool water splashed onto Ronan and Francie as the fish landed in the water and then flew out of it again. She watched them for a minute, continuing to move her fingers underwater. Then she pulled her hand up and looked at Ronan. He was staring at her, eyes wide.

"How did you do that?" he asked, his voice in a whisper.

"It's easy," she replied. "You just stick your hands in the water and wiggle your fingers around. Here, I'll show you." She did it again, but more slowly. This time, the fish jumped more slowly out of the water, but still put on the same show.

"You try it," she said.

Ronan stuck his hand in and followed what Francie had done. The water remained still.

"Where'd you learn how to do that?" he asked her.

Francie didn't respond. She felt that it wouldn't be a good idea to mention Sylvie.

"I—I don't really know," Francie said. "I just kind of did it." She wrapped her hands around her legs, not daring to touch the water again. Ronan stared at the water.

"Do it again," he insisted.

She shook her head. "No. You think it's weird."

"I think it's cool," he replied. "I want to figure out how to do it." Francie looked at him. Suddenly she knew that Ronan wouldn't be able to make the fish jump in the air, no matter how long she tried to teach him.

"Maybe another time," she said, standing up.

Francie made her way up the trail with Ronan following her. The hot sun soon dried their wet clothing. They didn't talk much and Francie kept biting her nails, an uneasy feeling stirring in her stomach. When they were almost home, she stopped suddenly and turned to Ronan.

"Do you think Sylvie is a witch?" she asked.

"Why?"

"I just want to know."

"Some people say she is. My dad doesn't get along with her too good because she's always in his business about hunting and all that. One time he told me he thought she was a witch, but I don't think he meant for real," Ronan replied, his voice quiet. He kicked a pebble with his shoe.

"Augustus thinks she is," Francie said.

Ronan looked up and laughed. "Augustus asked your grandma to marry him 'bout forty times. He probably thinks she's a witch just because she's so mean to him!"

This time it was Francie's turn to stare, surprised.

"He did? How do you know?"

"Everyone here knows everything about everyone, that's how."

"Well why is she mean to him then?" Francie asked.

"I dunno," Ronan admitted. "Maybe because she's a witch." He gave her a crooked smile that told Francie that Ronan didn't believe that was true. Francie turned around and began walking up the hill toward Sylvie's. With this new information about Sylvie and Augustus, she stopped thinking about the fish. Instead, she started thinking about how Sylvie lived all alone all year round and how perfect it would be if Sylvie and Augustus got married.

"I'm getting allowance tomorrow," she told Ronan, when they got to the road. "Let's go get ice cream in the afternoon."

"Sure," Ronan replied. "Plus, my sister leaves this afternoon so starting then, you get a free bike for two weeks!" And with that, he picked his bike up from Sylvie's driveway and biked home.

Chapter 9

The next morning, as Francie was helping Sylvie sort herbs at the table, Ronan knocked on the door. Francie recognized his quick pounding knock immediately, especially since no one else ever came to the house. But Ronan had never come to the house in the morning before.

"Hey, anyone in there?" he shouted.

Sylvie stood up and opened the door.

Ronan stood there, smiling from ear to ear.

"I have something for Francie," he said. He was holding his sister's bike. "I know it's kinda early, but my mom and dad said I didn't have to do chores today and I just wanted to give this to her."

Sylvie looked at Francie, who bit her lip to keep from looking too excited.

"Why don't you take the morning off, Francie? Go ride into town. Just come back for lunch," she said.

"Thank you!"

Francie raced out the door and then saw Ronan's bike on the ground.

"You brought both the bikes up here? How?" she asked.

"It wasn't easy. You owe me one," he replied, hopping on his bike.

Francie grabbed his sister's bike. It was small and decorated with Disney princesses (which Francie had long since grown out of) but she didn't care. It was a bike and for the next two weeks it was hers.

Minutes later, they were flying down the dirt road. When they got into town, they realized that only the coffee shop was open.

"It's not like I want ice cream this early anyway," Ronan said. "Let's just ride around."

They started back up the hill, but Francie stopped when they got to the Fortune Gold Mining Museum.

"I wonder if there's anything about Sylvie's great-grandparents in there," she said.

"That place hasn't been open for years," Ronan replied, circling her on his bike.

"Oh."

"Why do you care about some stupid museum anyway?"

"It's just that my grandmother said something about her great-grandparents starting Fortune and I want to read about it."

He stopped. Then he smiled his crooked smile. "Just cuz it's closed doesn't mean we can't go in."

They both instinctively looked around the street. It was even quieter than usual. There weren't even any tourists on the porch of Bald Mountain Coffee Shoppe.

"How would we get in?" Francie asked, eyeing the building.

"C'mon," Ronan was already ahead of her, biking up the road. He hopped off next to the town hall and began walking his bike through the weeds between the town hall and the museum. Francie followed. They leaned their bikes against a tall pine that couldn't be seen from the road. Francie shivered when she looked at the woods behind the building, which suddenly seemed creepy to her. Or maybe her shiver came from knowing that they were about to do something they shouldn't.

The back of the museum looked much like the front, with a taped-over window and door, locked with a padlock. Ronan jiggled the lock.

"Looks like we're going in through the window."

The window was well above both of their heads.

"Okay, I'll hold you up and then you climb in through the window," Ronan said.

"What, just break through the glass? It doesn't look like it's all that broken."

They both stared at it.

"Got any better suggestions?" Ronan asked.

"Hey, this was your idea."

"You're the one who wants to go in the stupid museum!"

"Okay, okay. Hold me up and I'll see what I can do."

Francie lifted up her foot and Ronan put his hand under it, pushing her upwards. He groaned under her weight.

"Try to be quick. You weigh like ten million pounds."

Francie grabbed onto the ledge of the window and pulled herself towards it. The window was so covered with tape that she couldn't see inside. She tried pulling off the tape, but it was stuck.

"I don't know…" she said. Then she put her fingernails under the window and decided to give opening it a try. To her surprise, the window creaked ever so slightly open. Dust and dry paint blew into her eyes. She wiped them with the back of one hand and then tried pushing the window up further. It moved some more. She pushed until the window was halfway open, wide enough for both of them to crawl through.

"I can't hold you up anymore," Ronan moaned.

"It's okay, I think I got it." Francie grabbed onto the window sill and pulled herself inside. She landed with a thump on the floor and saw nothing but darkness. She waited for her eyes to adjust, but then heard Ronan down below. She leaned out the window as far as she could with her feet on the ground and tried to pull Ronan up.

"Just so you know, you weigh twenty million pounds," she told him, letting go. They tried again and this time he managed to grab onto the window sill. Soon the two of them stood inside the museum, their eyes blinking in the dark room. Ronan sneezed twice from the dust.

"Shhh," Francie told him. They looked at each other without moving. "What do you think would happen if someone caught us in here?"

"Oh probably just cut off our heads or something like that," Ronan joked, but he didn't sound as confident as usual.

"Well, we're in here. I guess we might as well look around," she whispered.

The museum was made up of one large room, with glass covered cases full of artifacts lining the wall. Above them were black and white photographs in wooden frames, so dusty that Francie had to wipe each one off with her sleeve to see the picture underneath. She walked toward the front door, aware of every creak in the wooden floor, so that she could start from the beginning.

Under the photograph nearest the door it read, "First miners in Fortune. Circa 1858" on a yellowed index card taped to the wall. The picture showed six pale men, all in wide-brimmed dark hats with long, bushy beards. They wore light-colored shirts, rolled up to their elbows and dark pants and boots. Each had a roll that looked like a sleeping bag tucked under one arm. Three of the men held shovels in their other hands and three held pans. A covered wagon stood to their left. None of them were smiling.

Francie looked more closely at the photograph. One of these men had to be Sylvie's great-grandfather. She wanted to look more closely at their faces, to feel recognition, some sort of resemblance that would tell her that he was related. But the dark room and blurry photograph made it impossible for her to see such details.

"Awesome," Ronan said from the other side of the room. "Look at this picture of a guy with a mountain lion."

Francie walked over to Ronan. A man, wearing the same gold-mining clothes as the men in the first picture, stared out at her from the photograph, his arm slung around a large mountain lion. Francie immediately thought of the mountain lion on the road and felt another jolt of electricity through her veins.

"That's my relative," she whispered.

"Franklin Wald, founder of Fortune," Ronan read. "Seems like that's the guy."

Francie gently lifted the photograph off of the nail and brought it over to the window to take a better look. Thick, tangled curls hung from under the man's hat. Francie fingered her own frizzy curls. His gaze was calm, even with his arm around a dangerous wild animal. Francie wondered about him. *Why was he so brave?*

"Say, that's pretty cool," Ronan said. "If your grandma's great-granddad started Fortune, that kind of makes you Queen of Fortune or something like that."

"That means you better start doing what I tell you," Francie laughed, looking up from the picture.

"Hey, come over and look at this one too. I think it's the same guy but he's got his family with him here. Maybe it's Sylvie's great-grandma or something. It says 'Wald family' underneath."

Francie walked back over, hanging the first photograph up again. The next picture showed a man, woman and five children standing in front of a small stone house. The photograph was taken from the bottom of steep stone steps leading up to the house. Francie had to look twice to recognize Sylvie's great-grandfather. He had shaved his beard and now wore a long mustache. Instead of his gold-mining clothes, he wore a dressier vest buttoned up under a coat and a shorter-brimmed hat. Yet she recognized the calm gaze from the other picture. Sylvie's great-grandmother stood next to him. Even with the stern expression on her face ("Why didn't anyone smile in those days?" Ronan asked), Francie could tell she was beautiful. Something about her cheeks and mouth reminded Francie of her mother. Francie wanted to ask her, "How did you feel about coming here? What made you agree to bring all of your children out to this wilderness and start a new life?"

Before she could look more carefully at the children in the photograph, the loud rumble of a truck outside filled the room. She and Ronan looked at each other.

"People are probably starting to come downtown," Ronan whispered. "Maybe we should go."

Francie nodded reluctantly.

Ronan eased himself out of the window first. Now that Francie was thinking again about people catching them in the museum, he seemed to land with a much louder sound than he should have. She hurriedly climbed out of the window. As she did, her arm caught on a nail sticking out from the window sill. A searing pain shot through her body.

"Ouch!" she yelled.

"Shhh! Do you want everyone to know we're here?" Ronan called from below.

She dropped to the ground and grabbed her arm.

"Oh man Francie, look at your arm!"

They both looked at the blood trickling down the side of her arm from between her fingers. Ronan took off his t-shirt and handed it to Francie.

"Put this on it," he said.

They both sat down and leaned against the building, listening to the birds and an occasional car driving by on the road in front of the building. After a few minutes, she pulled his t-shirt away and the bleeding had stopped.

"I don't think it's that bad," she said.

Ronan put back on his t-shirt and then hoisted her up so that she could close the window.

Chapter 10

I want to find that house," Francie told Ronan as they walked back to the bikes.

"What house?"

"The house from the picture of the Wald family. It's stone. It has to be here still. Somewhere in these woods."

Ronan grabbed his bike.

"OK. Where do we start though? It could take us years to look all around these woods."

Francie hopped onto her bike.

"Yeah, that's true." She felt discouraged. "But maybe someone knows about it."

"Yeah, maybe your grandmother?"

Francie thought about that for a minute. Sylvie might know, but for some reason she felt like she wouldn't want her asking about it.

"The co-op is open by now. Let's go get ice cream," she said. "My grandmother gave me allowance this morning and I told you yesterday that I'd get us some."

They left their bikes outside the co-op and walked over to the ice cream cooler. Francie picked out strawberry and Ronan picked out chocolate. They brought them up to the counter.

"How is your grandma doing, Francie?" Augustus asked, opening up the register.

"She's fine."

"That's good. That's good to hear," he said, as usual. Then he looked up at Ronan and Francie again. "You guys sure are dirty."

Francie looked over at Ronan and was torn between fear that Augustus would know what they had been doing and an urge to laugh. Ronan's shirt was smeared with blood and his white-blonde hair had turned gray with dust. His hand on his ice cream cone looked even grimier than usual.

"Francie, your arm is bleeding!" Francie had never heard Augustus speak so loudly before. She looked at her arm and saw that the blood had started trickling down it again. She was grateful for the interruption.

"Do you have any Band-Aids?" she asked.

Augustus walked to the back of the store and came back with a large Band-Aid. Francie handed Ronan her cone so that she could put it on.

"You better go back to your grandmother so she can clean that up," Augustus said. "Soon as you finish that cone."

Francie nodded in agreement. She thought he was overreacting a bit, but it was probably getting close to lunchtime and she had said she'd be home by then anyway.

"Sure. Thanks Augustus."

"Anytime. Just promise me you'll go get that cut cleaned up."

"I will. Say, do you know anything about a stone house around here?" Francie asked. She didn't dare to look at Ronan, feeling somehow they'd give away their morning's mission.

"A stone house?"

"Yeah, a really old one. My grandmother mentioned there is an old stone house around here somewhere. Belonged to relatives of mine, I think," Francie felt bad lying, especially after Augustus's concern about her cut, but she wasn't sure how else to explain that she knew about the house.

Augustus rubbed his chin.

"I've heard of that. Never seen it. It's way up on the west side of Bald mountain." He looked closely at Francie. "Why?"

"I'm just wondering."

"Well, you kids shouldn't be going up there without an adult or really even at all. There've been rock slides on that side of the mountain and it's not safe."

"Yeah, we won't go up there," Francie said. Augustus didn't look convinced.

"Plus the last time someone went hiking up there, he got attacked by a mountain lion. Barely made it down the mountain to get help because he lost so much blood."

Francie nodded and took her ice cream cone back from Ronan.

"Don't worry about us, Augustus. Thanks for the Band-Aid and the ice cream," Francie said.

"You kids be safe," he replied, looking at Francie. "Your grandmother would be mighty upset if anything ever happened to you."

"Told ya he's in love with your grandmother," Ronan whispered as they ate their ice cream outside.

"Why does telling us to be safe have anything to do with that?"

"Didn't you hear him? 'Your grandmother would be mighty upset...'" Ronan imitated Augustus' gravelly voice. Francie snorted, causing the ice cream to go up her nose. Ronan looked at her and then they both laughed until they were gasping for breath.

"Anyway," Ronan said when their laughter subsided, "that mountain lion attack must've been years ago. I've never heard about it. I'm sure people have gone up there since then. Plus, there are mountain lions everywhere up here in the mountains. I told you how one of them keeps getting into my dad's chickens."

Francie licked the ice cream that had dripped onto her hand. She could taste dust and blood.

"Should we go up tomorrow afternoon?" she asked.

"Works for me," Ronan replied, wiping his hands off on his jeans. As Francie finished her cone she wondered what her mother would think about her daughter shrugging off rock slides and mountain lions to go find a house in the woods. They grabbed their bikes and headed up the road.

Chapter 11

By the time Francie got home, her Band-Aid was soaked through with blood. Sylvie asked her what had happened. "Oh, I just fell off my bike," Francie replied, thinking that she'd lied more today than ever before in her life.

"You did?" Sylvie examined the cut.

"I guess my life in the country uses up more Band-Aids than my life in Studio City," Francie attempted a casual shrug and smile.

"It looks like something punctured it."

"Well, I think I landed on a rock."

"Hmmm. In any case, I'm going to call your mom to make sure you're up to date on your tetanus shots. But first let's clean it up and I'll put some herbs on it to soothe it and prevent infection."

Sylvie gently wiped the cut off with a warm washcloth and then handed Francie a clean rag to hold over it. She went to the kitchen and began pulling down different herbs and jars of spices, making a paste out of garlic, turmeric powder and black plum bark.

"This should help stop the bleeding and prevent infection," she explained to Francie as she applied the paste. Francie's arm had begun to throb and she was grateful for Sylvie's care.

After Sylvie had talked to Francie's mom, she handed the phone to Francie.

"Are you sure you're alright there, Francie?" Her mom asked, over and over again. "I just feel so terrible. The mountain lion and now this…"

59

Francie reassured her mom that everything was fine. She still felt sharp pangs of homesickness when she talked to her, but she realized that after a day of lying, she was telling her mother the truth.

- - -

That night, Francie sat at the table by the window and wrote on the postcard with the photo of the gold mine museum on the front.

Jenny - You wouldn't believe the adventures I'm having. I saw a picture of my great-great-great-grandpa and he was sitting next to a mountain lion! Me and my friend Ronan are going to find his house up in the woods. I'll tell you all about it when I see it.
XO, Francie

When she went to sleep, Francie dreamed again of Jenny's pool. This time she wasn't a bird, but she was herself, swimming in the water with the fish. It was beautiful and calm under the water and she admired their silver gills. Then she surfaced from the water to breathe and found herself face to face with the mountain lion from the road. The lion made a low growling noise that seemed to Francie to be some kind of warning. She immediately dove back into the water and then woke up, gasping for air.

Chapter 12

The next day, Francie spent the morning helping Sylvie around the garden. She chewed on some peppermint as she weeded. After a couple of weeks of Sylvie's instruction, she knew most of the herbs in the garden and knew which ones to nibble on as she worked or to clip when Sylvie asked for seasoning for bean soup. She found herself eating foods she never would have considered before. Everything tasted better when she picked it herself.

As she was weeding, Francie heard a crash at the house. She and Sylvie looked up. At first Francie didn't notice anything, but then she saw something rust-colored quivering on the windowsill.

"Sylvie, I think it's a robin!" she yelled. Sylvie stood up and ran with Francie over to the windowsill. The robin had stopped quivering and lay still by the time they reached it.

"It died," Francie cried, her eyes filling with tears.

Sylvie reached out and carefully picked up the robin.

"He's not dead," she replied to Francie. "Here, feel his heartbeat."

Francie placed her finger on the robin's soft chest as Sylvie indicated. Sure enough, she could feel the quick flutter of his heart.

Suddenly, the robin stirred. He stood up in Sylvie's hand and looked at the two of them with his head cocked to the side, as if to say, "What's all the fuss?" Then he opened his wings and flew away.

"They fly into the windows sometimes," Sylvie sighed. "He just sees the reflection of the sky and the trees and thinks it's real."

"Will he be okay?"

"He'll be fine," Sylvie replied. She smiled at Francie and surprised her by squeezing her hand. The robin had felt something healing in the warmth of Sylvie's hand and Francie felt it too.

Chapter 13

Ronan came by on his bike in the afternoon and they headed up the road to find the stone house. They weren't sure exactly which trail to take, but rode their bikes to a trail that seemed to go in the general direction of Bald Mountain.

They left their bikes by the side of the road and began to hike. After twenty minutes of hiking, it started to rain.

"Rain doesn't bother me," Ronan said.

"Me neither," replied Francie.

Another minute passed and suddenly the rain turned hard. Francie felt like someone was throwing sharp rocks at her face and arms. She closed her eyes and shielded her face.

"Hail does though!" Ronan yelled.

"What is going on? Is this supposed to happen in the summer?" Francie asked.

"C'mon, turn around! Let's go!" Ronan's voice was lost in the noise of cracking branches and hail pounding into the ground. Francie watched as he turned and began to run. She followed. They ran along the trail until they got to the road.

"Ride to my house!" Ronan yelled. "It's closer to here!"

Francie tried to ride but the hail jabbed into her face even harder on the bike. She put both her feet down and watched through squinted eyes as Ronan biked down the road. The hail came at her from all directions—falling from the sky and bouncing up at her from the road. She began to pedal again to keep up with Ronan, dodging the balls of ice as well as she could.

When they arrived at Ronan's house, battered and cold, his father's truck was in the driveway. Ronan pulled open the door, bracing to hold it open against the wind. Francie sighed with relief once she had escaped the wind and hail. She looked in surprise at her surroundings. While Ronan and Sylvie's houses looked similar from the outside, from the inside they couldn't have looked or felt more different. Sylvie's house was decorated in wood, old cloth, colored jars and plants, and the only sounds, aside from those that Sylvie and Francie made, came from the tea kettle or from the animals or wind outside. Ronan's house was cluttered with empty beer and soda cans, toys, heaps of clothing, mail, and dirty plates on almost every surface she could see. The noise of the television replaced the noise of the hail. Francie realized that in the weeks since she had arrived at Sylvie's, she hadn't once watched television or even seen one.

A man sat on the couch in front of the television, a cigarette in one hand and the remote in the other. He had short, spiky red hair. You could see his sunburned scalp underneath. He turned around to look at the two of them.

"Hey there Missy. Are you Ronan's fancy Hollywood girlfriend I've been hearing about?" He laughed until it turned into a cough.

"Dad! She's not my girlfriend."

Francie blushed.

"Naw, I'm just joking. Ro, buddy, I'm home from work for the day." He stood up, crushing his cigarette in an ashtray on the table and turning off the television. "Hard to work on a roof when it's hailing. Figured we could go get a pizza in town if you want. You can bring your…friend."

With the television off, Francie could hear that the hail had stopped. A steady rain made for a calmer noise above her.

"I'm Jim, by the way," Ronan's dad said, extending a rough but warm hand to Francie. "Do you wanna come get pizza?" he asked. He had Ronan's same crooked smile.

"Well...I probably would have to ask my grandmother first."

"You live with Sylvie, right? I'll give her a call." Before Francie could comment further, Jim had made plans to drop her off at Sylvie's in an hour, after pizza.

- - -

Like much of Fortune, Joe's Pizza had seen better days. The cracked floors, sticky plastic tablecloths and stained walls might have implied that the food wouldn't be top quality. To Francie, the gooey cheesy pizza couldn't have tasted any better. She realized that, along with television, she hadn't had pizza since arriving in Fortune. In Studio City, her mom ordered pizza so often that she grew tired of it. But after nearly a month away, she had started to miss it.

Jim asked her about her life in Studio City—What movie stars had she met? What are the people like out there? Is everyone in California as crazy as they seem? He asked her if she thought Fortune was the most boring place in the world or what.

"No, I really haven't been bored at all," she replied between bites.

"Francie saw a mountain lion on the road," Ronan said. "That's kind of exciting, huh?"

"You saw a mountain lion?" Jim asked.

"On the way up the road to my house—my grandmother's house," Francie replied. "I was walking up there, not paying attention..."

"What time of day was it?"

"Middle of the day..."

65

"That's not right. Probably the same stupid mountain lion that keeps getting into my chickens. You gotta be real careful," he warned. "You should see the way that lion turns the chicken coop into a mess of blood and feathers. Don't screw around, you hear me? Those things can kill you, just like that." He snapped his fingers.

Francie nodded, thinking of the mountain lion in her dream.

"Don't worry though. If I catch the mountain lion anywhere near my property, I'll blow its head off, just like that." He snapped again and laughed.

Francie suddenly felt queasy and wondered if she had eaten the pizza too fast.

"'Course your grandmother will probably try to blow my head off when I do. She's always talking crazy about how important the mountain lions are up here. Balance and all that."

Francie looked down at her plate. She was relieved when he changed the subject and started talking about their trip to Ronan's aunt's house.

"Say, Francie," Jim suddenly said, interrupting himself, "speaking of the chickens, would you mind coming by to take care of them when we're gone?"

"What do I need to do?"

"Feed them and collect their eggs. Then you drop the eggs off at the co-op right here every morning. You can keep all the money Augustus will give you for the eggs."

She hesitated. "I think that'd be alright."

"Don't worry about my mountain lion comments," he said, "It's been a couple weeks at least. And anyway, I've added another layer of chicken wire. I've got about five layers of wiring on there. Chicken wire, goat wire, pig wire, I don't even know what. You won't have a problem with that."

Jenny - Guess what I'll be doing this week? Taking care of chickens! Bet you didn't think I'd turn into a farmer this summer! XO, Francie

When Francie finished writing the postcard, she fingered her blue beaded necklace from Jenny and smiled, trying to imagine Jenny's reaction to reading about Francie the chicken farmer.

Chapter 14

It rained every afternoon for the next week. The rain itself wouldn't have stopped Francie and Ronan from trying to find the stone house, but the thunder and lightning did. Sylvie drove Francie to Ronan's house most afternoons. She learned how to take care of the chickens, who clucked at her heels and made her laugh with their bobbing heads and fat bodies. Otherwise they spent most of their afternoons playing cards—Go Fish, Old Maid, or War, until they grew tired of those and made up their own card games.

On the first sunny afternoon, Francie waited outside for Ronan to meet her at Sylvie's. Sylvie called her in to let her know that Ronan was on the phone.

"Bad news," he told her. "I can't come up today. I gotta go to my aunt's this week instead of next week. My dad has a construction project that starts next week so we have to go early if we're going to go see my aunt."

Francie sighed, trying to imagine what she'd do for a whole week without Ronan to explore with in the afternoons.

"Hey, you still there?" he asked.

"Yeah, yeah. That stinks… Well, have fun at your aunt's house."

"Are you gonna keep looking for the house?"

"Maybe. I don't know. Maybe I'll wait until you get back."

"Yeah. You can borrow my bike if you want. The shed's always open. Just come down and grab it when you want."

"Thanks."

"Tell her not to forget about the chickens!" Jim yelled in the background.

"I'll remember the chickens."

"You remember where the key is, right?"

"Under the rock by the back door."

"Yup. Later Francie."

"Have a fun trip."

She hung up the phone.

"Everything okay, Francie?" Sylvie asked.

"Yeah, it's fine. Ronan's just going away this week instead of next week. I might go down now and get his bike."

"Do you want me to drive you down?"

"No, no, that's okay. I'm going to ride Rosie's bike down there and trade it for Ronan's for the week."

Francie rode quickly. She hoped Ronan would still be there when she arrived but the driveway was empty when she got there. She knocked on the door just in case, but no one answered. She walked over to the shed and pulled out Ronan's bike, thinking to herself that at least she'd have the right-sized bike for a week.

She was about to get on the bike when she heard a crash and then frantic high-pitched sounds from the chicken coop. She put the bike down on the ground. She didn't need to feed them until tomorrow, but she felt she ought to check on them. She breathed a sigh of relief when she found them all pecking away at the ground, ruffling their feathers and walking around comically, as usual.

"Silly chickens," she said. "Don't scare me like that."

She turned around and began to walk back to her bike. When she was almost there, she stopped, her breath catching in her throat.

The mountain lion stood between her and the bike. She recognized the scar and knew it was the same mountain lion she had seen before. She thought of Sylvie instructing her not to run. She thought of the photograph of Sylvie's great-grandfather with his arm slung around the mountain lion. She thought of Ronan's dad, describing the blood and feathers in their yard.

"Please don't kill me," she whispered. She began to shake. Her hands, her legs, even her head shook. She took a deep breath and looked up at the mountain lion. The mountain lion looked back at her. She felt the same jolt of electricity she had felt before when her eyes met the mountain lion's stare. Her shaking stopped, though her heart still pounded in her chest, in her ears.

The mountain lion moved to the right, never dropping her gaze. Francie inched to the left, closer to the bike. She walked slowly, reminding herself to breathe. The mountain lion moved slowly too, away from the bike.

When Francie got to the bike, she grabbed it and swung her leg over it. She was about to pedal when she noticed something behind the mountain lion. A smaller lion, with large paws and bigger ears peered up at her. Its eyes were a bright dandelion yellow and its fur fuzzy and spotted. A cub. The cub looked curiously at Francie, turning its head to the side. Francie took it in for a moment, forgetting the danger of the situation. The mountain lion was a mother. She had been feeding the chickens to her baby.

As soon as she thought of the chickens, she thought of Ronan's dad again and began to pedal as fast as she could. Her lungs burned for air and legs ached. But once again, she didn't stop or look back until she reached Sylvie's house. When she got there, she threw the bike down and collapsed in the grass. She heard nothing but the gasp of her breath and drum of her heart as she lay on the ground. She closed her eyes and pictured the mountain lion. The sun warmed her face and the danger felt more distant.

She decided that Sylvie might wonder about her lying in the grass and got up to go inside, wanting Sylvie's reassurance again that she had no reason to fear the mountain lion. The house was empty and

Sylvie's boots weren't by the door. Francie walked into the garden and greenhouse, but didn't find her there either. She heard singing in the distance and paused to listen. Drawn to the sound, she followed it into the woods.

Chapter 15

Francie continued to follow the noise, which led her deeper and deeper into the woods. After walking for ten minutes, she stopped, and considered that, aside from walking or biking on the road to Ronan's, she had never spent any time alone in the wilderness before. The woods, which looked so dark from Sylvie's cabin, were actually dappled in sunlight now that she stood in them. She recognized the wild raspberries on the bushes to her right and wondered if that's where Sylvie picked them for her jam. She had never walked this way with her before.

She continued down the path until it dropped off steeply at the edge of a creek bank. The sound was louder here. She looked down and caught her breath. Sylvie sat on a rock by the creek, her arms wrapped around her knees and her long gray hair loose down her back. Her eyes were closed and she was singing. Hundreds of birds surrounded her. Francie had never seen so many colors in one place before—bright blues, pale yellows, iridescent greens, almost every shade of brown or gray imaginable. They flew over and around Sylvie in a beautiful dance. They echoed her singing with their own voices.

Remembering Sylvie's reaction when Francie had commented on the fish, Francie drew back and stood behind a tree. She thought of running back to the cabin before Sylvie could see her, but the music held her captive. She sat down, leaning against the bark, and listened. Sylvie didn't sing in words, but hummed and whistled a tune that blended in with the sounds of the wind in the trees, the rushing water and the singing birds.

As she sat, a sense of calmness replaced Francie's fear. Lulled by the music, she settled against the tree trunk and leaned her head back, looking up at the blue sky through the pine needles. The ground under the pine tree was soft with layers of pine needles and after a while, Francie drifted off to sleep.

She dreamed that, instead of her grandmother, Francie was singing by the creek, surrounded by hundreds of dancing birds. She was caught up in the energy of the birds, watching all of their colors fly by, when she noticed something on the bank above her. She looked up and the birds immediately froze in mid-air. Above her stood the mountain lion. As in Francie's other dream, the mountain lion let out a low growl, as if in warning.

Francie woke up to find herself in the dark. It took her a minute to remember why she was lying against a tree in the woods. She stood up.

"Sylvie?" she called, hesitantly. She took a step to peer over the edge of the river bank, but in the dark missed the step and her foot slipped from under her. She landed on her bottom and slid down until her hiking boot splashed into the creek. She stood up, pulling her foot out of the water. Her foot felt heavy and stuck to the mud. Francie wrenched it free. Though she could barely see, Sylvie obviously was no longer there. For the second time that day, Francie began to shake out of fear. It had taken her at least ten minutes to walk to the creek in the daylight and now, in the dark, she couldn't imagine how she would stay on the trail.

"Well, sitting here won't get you home," she said out loud to herself. She pulled herself up the muddy bank, her hands slipping into the cool mud. It took several attempts and twice she slid all the way back to the bottom, scraping her knees on rocks on the way down.

When she got to the top, she was relieved to see that the moonlight had made its way through the trees and, while she couldn't see perfectly, she had better vision than she had by the creek.

As she walked, she kept thinking of the mountain lion at Ronan's house and the mountain lion in her dreams. An owl let out a low cry from the trees above her and Francie began to run. Finally, she saw the lights from Sylvie's cabin. She ran through the garden and once again arrived at Sylvie's house muddy and covered in scrapes.

Sylvie hugged her when she came in.

"I was starting to get worried about you," she said. She looked Francie over. "And I suppose I should have been. How did you get so beat up this time?"

Francie wanted to tell Sylvie about the mountain lion, to ask her about the birds, to talk to her about her strange dreams and how she had fallen asleep in the woods and woken up scared. But, despite her nap, she felt completely exhausted. Sylvie seemed to understand.

"Never mind for now, let's get you cleaned up." She ran a warm bath for Francie and added some lavender to the water. Francie eased herself in and lay back.

"I'll make you some tea!" Sylvie called from the other room.

When Francie was cleaned up, she and Sylvie sat at the table in their pajamas—a t-shirt and sweat pants for Francie and worn flannel pajamas for Sylvie—and sipped the chamomile tea with honey.

"Why don't you worry about me in the woods?" Francie finally asked. Sylvie stirred her tea.

After a while she replied, "I worried about you when it started getting dark and you weren't home."

"But I mean, you let me go off by myself even though you know there are mountain lions and bears and stuff out there…"

"Do you think that I shouldn't let you go?"

"No, it's just…it's just that I don't know why you weren't more worried when I saw a mountain lion before. Ronan's dad said I should be scared. He told me how one keeps tearing the chickens apart."

"Mountain lions can be dangerous," Sylvie murmured. She seemed to stare out the window, though when Francie looked she only could see their reflection shining off of the dark glass. Francie thought back to the afternoon at the table with her mom, right before her mother told her about her summer plans. She decided that Sylvie had something she needed to tell her but didn't think Francie would want to hear.

Sylvie turned to her.

"Francie," she said, "I think that I should tell you something."

Francie waited.

"Do you remember when we went to the creek and the fish danced in the air?" Sylvie asked.

Francie nodded. Of course she remembered.

"Fish don't normally do that," Sylvie continued. "When other people go there, the fish swim quietly at the bottom of the creek or else they hide behind rocks and don't show themselves at all."

"What does that have to do with mountain lions?" Francie asked.

"I can communicate with animals in a way that most people can't," Sylvie said. She looked down into her steaming mug and took a deep breath. "You can too, Francie. I saw that in you when we were by the creek that day."

"But I didn't know that fish don't just do that," Francie replied stubbornly.

"You felt a certain energy from the fish in the water. An energy that connected them to you and that allowed you to tell them, through the simple movement of your hand, to put on such a beautiful show." Sylvie stated this rather than asking Francie if it was true.

"Is that bad?" Francie asked. She thought of Sylvie's face at the creek that day and how she had practically closed the door in Francie's face when they had returned to the cabin.

"I don't think so," Sylvie replied slowly. "But people aren't always comfortable with people who are different. Most people can't do that so it's not something that everyone considers normal. Because of that, I am not always eager to share my ability with others."

"I still don't really get it," Francie replied.

"Francie, I've scared some people before by having such an unusual connection with nature." Sylvie paused. "I didn't know if it would scare you and that's why I didn't talk to you about it. But I think that it's important for you to know that you are safe when you see a mountain lion in the woods."

"I still don't really see how that makes me safe."

"The ability to sense the energy of those fish and to harness that energy is a gift, really. You can communicate with the animals out there in the forest in a way that others can't. The mountain lion won't hurt you because of the energy that the two of you share. It's a matter of deep trust."

Francie thought about Sylvie's great-grandfather, sitting with his arm slung around a mountain lion. She wanted to ask Sylvie about him. Had he had the same ability? But she didn't know how to ask without revealing that she and Ronan had spent the morning sneaking into the Fortune Gold Mining Museum.

She thought back to Sylvie's comment that Augustus thought she was a witch. Ronan had quickly dismissed it, but suddenly Francie felt scared. Did this ability mean that she was a witch after all? Did it mean that Francie was a witch?

"You don't need to be scared, Francie," Sylvie said, sensing Francie's sudden tension.

"I'm okay," she replied. "Just tired." She now felt anything but tired, but she was eager for the conversation to end.

Sylvie nodded.

"This is probably a lot for you to digest after a long day outside. Let's go to sleep and we can talk more in the morning,"

When Francie crawled into her cot, she wondered if she would be able to fall asleep after such a long nap in the woods. She lay listening to the sounds of crickets outside the cabin. She heard an owl and remembered her fear when she heard the owl in the woods.

"Are you still awake, Francie?" Sylvie asked.

"Yes."

"You never did tell me how you ended up all covered in mud in the woods."

"I saw you with the birds," Francie replied.

"Oh."

"And I fell asleep."

"I'm sorry if I scared you," Sylvie said after a while.

"No. I'm glad I saw you. It was beautiful. Sylvie?"

"Yes?"

"When did you first learn that you had…a gift?"

"I guess I've almost always known. Or as long as I can really remember. One of my first memories is from when I was about three years old. I was sitting on a stone wall at my great-grandfather's house. He was cracking walnuts and we'd sit there together, eating them. Some chipmunks came up, interested in the nuts. I saw them and laughed as they dashed around us. My great-grandfather turned to me and said, 'You can call to them Sylvie.' And so, I began calling. 'Here chippy chippy, here chippy chippy,'" Sylvie laughed at the memory.

"But he grinned and said, 'Not like that. You need to just feel their energy and let them feel yours, to let them know that they can trust you.' I was only three but somehow that made sense to me. I looked at the chipmunk and he came running over to me and ate a nut right out of my hand. My grandfather said to me, 'You have a gift, Sylvie.

Be careful how you use it and who you share it with.' It was the last time I saw him."

"What happened to him?" Francie asked.

"He passed away soon after that. He was old, it was his time." Sylvie replied. They were both quiet. Francie wondered if the stone wall was the same one he stood next to in the photograph of the stone house. As she tried to figure out how to ask Sylvie more about him without giving away her museum trip, she heard Sylvie begin to snore.

That night, Francie dreamed of birds flying overhead. She was sitting in the forest by the creek watching their colors, orchestrating a dance with her own voice. She looked up and saw Sylvie's great-grandfather walking down the creek bank toward her. He was trying to tell her something, but she couldn't hear what he said. Then, as she watched, he turned into a mountain lion. He opened his mouth to speak again, this time exposing long yellow teeth. Francie once again woke up in fright.

Chapter 16

The next morning, Francie woke up early and rode to Ronan's to feed the chickens. She didn't mention the mountain lion she'd seen at Ronan's to Sylvie and, despite their talk, still felt nervous when she arrived at the house. She looked around cautiously as she walked to the chicken coop, but there was no sign of the mountain lion or her cub.

The chickens clucked and chattered as usual. She had never heard Ronan or his dad call them by any names, but she had come up with her own names for them, naming them all after the singers of the country music she often heard at Ronan's house and at the co-op. She talked to Dolly, Faith, LeeAnn and Shania as she took the eggs, wondering if being able to communicate with animals meant she could communicate with chickens. She giggled at the thought of the chickens flying around her in a beautiful dance and even waved her hand in the air once in imitation of Sylvie by the creek. The chickens looked unimpressed and Francie felt foolish.

After she collected the eggs and put them in cartons, she piled the cartons into a bag hanging on a nail in the coop. She carefully pulled the strap onto her shoulder, hoping that she could make it to the food co-op with any of the eggs intact. She rode slowly, aware of every hole and rock in the road.

She found Augustus in the back of the food co-op, sorting through early season peaches.

"I brought you some eggs," she said in greeting. "I rode as carefully as I could so I wouldn't break any." She dumped the bag down on the table next to Augustus, where it landed with a thud.

"Oh no!" she cried, placing her hands over her face. "I was so careful!" She peeked from behind her fingers and could see a tiny bit of liquid leaking out of the bottom of the bag. Augustus looked at her and they both started laughing.

"Let's see what we can salvage," he said, opening up the canvas sack. Fortunately, only three eggs in the bottom carton had cracked. "Not bad for surviving a bike ride and being slammed onto the table." He smiled. "You know what? No one's even going to be in here for another hour at least. What do you say we go next door for something to drink?"

Francie looked down at her egg-smeared hands.

"Go wash up in the back and we'll go on over."

Francie had never been inside the Bald Mountain Coffee Shoppe. Sylvie made it out to be almost exclusively for tourists, but when she walked inside she recognized several people she had seen before shopping at the food co-op when she and Ronan sat outside eating ice cream. The shop smelled like a soothing mix of cinnamon, coffee and chocolate. Augustus ordered himself a cup of black coffee and a cup of hot chocolate for Francie. The woman behind the counter smiled at Francie and asked her if she'd like whipped cream. Francie nodded and watched as she swirled a big dollop on top of Francie's drink.

"I've never been in here," Francie told Augustus as they sat down.

"Yeah, I guess your grandma probably doesn't like to go here too much. Bad memories maybe."

"What do you mean?"

Augustus looked surprised.

"You know that she and John owned this place, right?" He

gestured around the room with his free hand, holding his mug of coffee with the other.

Francie shook her head.

"I don't really know that much about my grandfather," she replied. "My mom never talked about him and with Sylvie, well I guess I've never asked."

"Well, he owned half this town really. Not that half this town is saying all that much!" Augustus grinned. "But he owned this and the gem shop and I guess the museum had been around for a while but he kind of ran it. Closed up when he left."

Francie looked across the street at the boarded up museum and wondered what Augustus would think if he knew that she knew exactly what it looked like inside.

"He was a business man from Denver. I don't think he ever pictured himself in a town like this, but he came through here and met your grandmother and I guess that was it."

Francie held her breath, hoping Augustus would continue.

"So anyway, when he came here, he just opened shop. The buildings were here but it was all run down and boarded up. He saw an opportunity with tourists coming through for hiking. Can't say it hurt my business either to have these around."

He looked out at the museum too and seemed lost in thought for a minute. He took a gulp from his mug, wiped the coffee off of his mustache and then looked at Francie.

"Well, should we get back to the eggs?" he asked, pushing his chair back.

"Wait, why did he leave?"

"That Francie, I do not know," he said. "And I probably will never understand. He just up and left one day. Never came back for all that I seen."

"But that doesn't make any sense," Francie argued stubbornly.

"Life doesn't promise to make any sense," he replied, standing up.

When Francie rode her bike back to Sylvie's, she thought over her conversation with Augustus. She kept thinking of Sylvie talking about how her gift had scared people. She hadn't pried Augustus further, but she felt that he knew something more. She decided that she'd get more information with her second egg delivery tomorrow.

Chapter 17

Francie arrived at the co-op with more eggs, hoping for another morning of conversation. She found Augustus surrounded by extra bins of vegetables and fruit.

"How's your grandmother?" he asked, but he seemed distracted.

"She's fine. But what's all this?"

"Just found out a whole busload of campers from Denver is coming through today. Gotta get everything ready," he told her.

"When will they be here?"

"'Bout an hour."

Augustus stood up.

Francie stared at him. For the first time since she'd met him, Augustus was wearing a t-shirt instead of a flannel. A thick, rope-like purple scar ran from his wrist all the way up to the sleeve of his t-shirt.

"What happened to you?" she asked.

He looked down at his arm.

"Help me unload these bins and I'll tell you a story," he said.

Francie began to unload a bin of strawberries onto the shelf. Augustus continued to move crates toward the front of the store. He didn't speak and after a while Francie wondered if he had forgotten about his story.

When she finished unloading the strawberries, Francie walked up to the front of the store. She heard voices outside and was surprised to see a crowd of about thirty teenagers standing in front of the door wearing bright yellow YMCA t-shirts. She had never seen so many people gathered in one place in Fortune. Augustus opened the door and they walked in, joking and laughing, new hiking boots squeaking against the floor. Francie soon found herself helping them fill bags with gorp, find bottles of water and juice, and pick out the freshest peaches to bring on their hike. She hadn't felt homesick in a few days, but seeing the crowd of kids laughing and talking together reminded her of her friends at home. She missed Jenny, missed her mom, and even missed the chaos and crowdedness of Studio City. When the teenagers left, silence settled back on the store like dust.

"Should we sit out front for a little bit?" Augustus asked.

He and Francie sat down. Francie was absorbed in thoughts of home, when Augustus began to speak.

"I've had this scar for a long time," he said. "I have a few of them actually. This one on my cheek and another on my left leg."

Francie waited.

"When I moved here, it was to get away. Seems to me that's the way with most people who live here. Either that, or their families have been here forever and they can't imagine life another way."

"Like Sylvie," Francie said. "Her family's been here a really long time."

"Exactly. I came about thirty years ago."

"So you've been here a really long time too."

Augustus chuckled. "You know, I guess it has been now. I didn't expect to stay this long. I just came to get away from the city and from my life at that time. I started working at this co-op, thinking I'd be here a year, maybe two. And then I fell in love."

He looked at Francie. "Only the woman I fell in love with, her husband had just left. She wasn't ready to meet someone new. I tried to talk to her and to be friends with her but she wasn't interested. I knew I would have to prove that I appreciated her so that she would trust me. And so I waited. And as I was waiting, the guy who used to run this store passed away. I took it over and kept myself busy, but I was really waiting for her.

"There was a place she used to go way up in the woods. She went there to get away from things I guess. I was foolish and I thought that maybe if I followed her up there I could talk to her. We would be away from everything—from the town, from her bad memories, from the judgment of other people..." He paused and looked down at his arm.

"So I followed her up there one day. I lost track of her though and got a little bit lost in the woods."

"I got lost in the woods one time," Francie said. "Were you scared?"

"No, not at first. I've done my fair share of hiking around here. But then I came to a point where I was surrounded by huge boulders and I had to either figure out a way to climb up one or to get down. Neither way looked that easy. I was stuck for a minute, trying to decide what to do and I saw a mountain lion on the rock above, looking down at me."

"A mountain lion?" Francie looked at the scar on his arm and thought of the mountain lion's yellow teeth.

"A mountain lion did this to me," he said. "Jumped down on me from a rock up above. The next thing I knew, he was on top of me, ripping me to shreds. Just about killed me. Probably would have too..."

Francie shuddered, shaking her head as if to erase the memory of standing so close to such a dangerous animal. She had been willing to believe Sylvie that she had a gift around animals, but after hearing Augustus's story, she doubted that she could ever make a connection with such a powerful beast.

"So how did you escape?" Francie asked. She felt short of breath, even though they were just sitting on a bench.

"I can't say that I really did. If she hadn't seen me, right at that moment, my bones would probably still be up there on that mountain. She called out to the mountain lion and the next thing I know, the mountain lion was gone. I still barely made it home, I had lost so much blood. She helped me of course. And, of course I did make it home, or I wouldn't be here telling you this story." He smiled at Francie. "I probably shouldn't be telling it to you anyway, scaring you like this."

"Oh, that's okay. I'm not scared," Francie tried to smile back.

"Well, anyway, she never did forgive me for following her up there or for nearly killing myself in those woods."

Augustus shook his head slightly and then stood up.

"I suppose I should get back to work," he said, even though both the store and street remained empty of people.

He stopped by the door. "I really don't mean to scare you, Francie. You just be careful in those woods, you know? Oh, and thank you for your help today."

"Sure, anytime."

Augustus closed the door behind him.

Chapter 18

Francie paused in front of the co-op door. She had her morning's carton of eggs with her, but she wondered if Augustus would want to see her today after she had caused him to dig up such unpleasant memories the day before. She contemplated turning around and biking back to Sylvie's, but of course there was the question of the eggs. She sighed and slowly pushed open the door.

She found Augustus in the back corner, arranging the postcards on the rack.

"I've sold more postcards since you arrived this summer than I probably have in all my years of running the co-op," he said by way of greeting.

Francie smiled in relief. "I haven't bought that many."

"I haven't sold that many," he laughed. "I might even have to have some more made up now. Who are you sending them to, if you don't mind my asking?"

"My friend Jenny," Francie responded. "She's my best friend in Studio City."

"That must be hard, being away from your best friend for the summer."

"Yeah," Francie said. She pointed to the necklace around her neck. "She gave me this when I left so I wouldn't forget her."

"A summer can feel like a long time," Augustus replied.

"I really miss her." Francie rubbed her hand along the beads of the necklace, thinking about playing Marco Polo in Jenny's pool and making up dance moves to their favorite Miley Cyrus song in her room. "But I do like it here more than I thought. And I didn't think I'd have any friends here, but I do. I didn't know I'd learn to ride a bike. I just had no idea what to expect. I didn't even know my grandmother, you know."

Augustus held a postcard out to Francie. She placed the eggs on a shelf and looked at the photograph on the front. It was the postcard of the woman in bell bottoms standing in a field of flowers.

"Speaking of your grandmother, you know who that is, right?" Augustus asked.

Francie studied the picture. She had sent the exact postcard to Jenny. She had noticed the brown bell bottoms and western shirt, but hadn't paid much attention to the woman's face. She had long brown hair, parted in the middle, and a shy smile with a chipped front tooth. Francie noticed a gold locket around her neck.

"No way!" she exclaimed. Augustus laughed.

"I have no idea how I convinced Sylvie to pose for me, but Fortune is not exactly overrun with models ready to pose for postcards. I think she took pity on me. I love this picture. There's no one in Fortune as pretty as your grandmother." His face turned a deep red. He looked away from Francie and began flipping through the other postcards. Francie studied the postcard more closely. Sylvie *was* beautiful in the picture. Not in a dazzling way like Francie's mother, but she had her own natural beauty.

"You took the pictures for the postcards?" Francie asked.

"I used to be a photographer, a long long time ago. Before I moved to Fortune. Now I just take pictures for fun. And for postcards every twenty years or so! I took all the pictures on the walls." He waved his hand in the general direction of the framed pictures.

Francie looked at the photograph of Bald Mountain on the wall and thought about the stone house, nestled under the trees somewhere on the vast mountain. She doubted she'd ever see it after Augustus's story the day before. She wondered if he thought about the mountain lion attacking him when he looked at the photograph on the wall.

- - -

On the way back to Sylvie's from the co-op, Francie noticed patches of dandelions in a small field alongside the road. She lay Ronan's bike in the grass just off the road and decided to pick some greens for Sylvie. She walked into the field and kneeled down, pulling off leaves and placing them in the bag she had used to carry the egg carton to the co-op. When the bag was almost full and she was about to stand up to leave, she heard a rustling noise in the grass in front of her. Her heart began to pound as she pictured the mountain lion's scarred face. She looked up and instead saw a brown rabbit with long ears looking at her curiously. She laughed out loud.

"You scared me!" she accused.

The rabbit tilted his head to the side and wiggled his nose. Francie held out her hand and he hopped over to her. She stroked his soft fur with one hand and held out a dandelion green for him in the other. He nibbled it from her hand and then hopped into her lap. Francie continued to pet him, wondering if she had ever felt anything as soft as his silky fur. She sat there for a while, petting the wild rabbit in a field of dandelion greens with the sun on her back. When a car drove by, the rabbit hopped away and Francie got back on Ronan's bike and rode back to Sylvie's.

- - -

At the corner table by the window, she pulled out a postcard from the pile in her dresser to send to Jenny. This time she carefully studied the picture, which was a close-up of a lavender, white and yellow flower. In purple print underneath it read: Rocky Mountain Columbine, Colorado State Flower. Instead of just seeing a photograph on a card, she couldn't help but imagine Augustus walking around Fortune and recording all of its natural beauty with his camera.

Jenny - Today I patted a bunny when I was picking dandelions. Did you know that you can eat dandelions? I had no idea. Oh, guess what? That last postcard I sent you? That's a picture of my grandmother! XO, Francie

Chapter 19

When Ronan returned, he was full of stories to tell. He caught a fish as big as his arm, drove an ATV all by himself, and learned how to do a flip off the dock at the lake. Francie was excited to have him back, but didn't tell him what she had seen or heard that week. Instead, she talked about the chickens—how she had named them and how she had to stop wearing flip flops because Dolly kept pecking her toes. Ronan told her that he couldn't wait to start looking for the house again now that all the storms had passed. Francie shrugged and said she didn't know if she felt up for a long hike anytime soon, but didn't offer any explanation why not.

Since Rosie was back too, it was difficult for them to get away on a hike anyway. Ronan's mom didn't want her wandering around in the woods and Ronan had to watch her most afternoons. She also insisted on riding her bike whenever Francie wanted to use it, which meant that Francie had to arrive everywhere on foot or else ride on the seat of Ronan's bike. They spent most afternoons at Ronan's house, playing cards or sliding down a mud path that they created with the hose and some dirt in the yard, much to Ronan's mom's horror.

One afternoon, right before Francie was about to return to Sylvie's, another hail storm rolled through, pounding Ronan's roof with fist-sized balls of ice. Ronan's mom called Sylvie and suggested that Francie stay for dinner. Ronan's dad would drop her off after they ate, as long as the hail had stopped. They started dinner by eating heaping plates of spaghetti with meatballs in front of the television, but when the power suddenly went out, Ronan's mom set up two candles on the living room table and they took turns telling ghost stories between bites. Ronan's dad told the scariest stories, about vengeful ghosts haunting the woods of Fortune, but Rosie's stories always ended with her yelling, "Boo!" as loud as she could, causing Francie to drop her fork each time. She started to hope the power wouldn't go back on so that Ronan's mom couldn't see the mess she'd made of the couch.

Then, as they ate, a large crashing sound came from outside. Ronan's mom explained that it was probably just a tree, hit by lightning or knocked over by the force of the wind. By the time they had finished dinner, the hail had stopped but the lights hadn't come back on. Rosie begged her parents for Francie to spend the night, but when her mom picked up the phone, the line was dead and they couldn't call Sylvie to let her know Francie wouldn't be home. Ronan's dad told her that he'd drive her home after checking to make sure the hail storm hadn't damaged the roof of the chicken coop.

As Ronan's dad fumbled in the dark for his coat and boots, Rosie began another story. Francie settled back on the couch, her stomach full and eyelids heavy. She felt a blast of cold air when Ronan's dad opened the door and she shivered, curling her legs up under her. The wind from the door blew out the candles and Rosie shrieked with delight, declaring that a ghost had blown them out. Francie yawned as Rosie continued to tell her nonsensical story about a haunted house full of witches who were scared of Halloween.

Suddenly, a sound like a loud clap filled the air. Francie screamed and her foot burned as if on fire.

Ronan's mom stood up. "Jim?" she yelled, as though her husband could hear her from outside.

Francie clutched her foot, moaning in agony.

"Are you alright?" Ronan asked.

His mother had run to the door and was yelling to his father outside.

Francie closed her eyes, trying to shut out the pain that continued to pierce her foot. She could feel tears on her cheeks, but didn't let go of her foot to wipe them away.

"Ronan, what's wrong with Francie?" Rosie asked.

Ronan's father came to the door.

"It's okay, Louann. No need to have a heart attack over a gun shot. Just some stupid mountain lions out in the chicken shed. The tree next to the shed fell over, knocking down part of the wiring and the lions got in there. I took a shot at them but I don't know if I got 'em or not. Looks like they got two of the chickens." He shook his head. His face was bright red, from cold or anger or both.

Francie whimpered, drawing attention from Ronan's parents for the first time.

"Mom, something's wrong with Francie," Ronan said.

"My foot…" she whispered. The initial shock of the pain had subsided, but she still felt a sharp throbbing in her foot and leg.

"Did something from the couch poke your foot, honey?" Ronan's mom asked. "God knows there's enough junk on that couch."

Francie shook her head.

"A foot cramp," Ronan's dad said authoritatively. "When you sit on your feet, you move all the blood out of them. Shake your foot around and it will feel better."

"Oh, I've had that before. Does it feel like you've got needles all over your foot?" Rosie asked.

It didn't but Francie nodded in agreement to prevent any more questions.

"I think I'd better go home," she whispered.

Ronan and his dad helped Francie to the truck. She sat in the back seat, nauseous from the smell of stale cigarette smoke, listening to Ronan's dad rant about the lions. He had to stop the truck three times so that he could move fallen trees and branches from the road. "What a night," he muttered each time he got back in the truck. By the time they got to Sylvie's, the power had returned. Francie sighed in relief at the sight of her grandmother's house, with soft yellow lights welcoming them from the windows.

"I think I can walk okay," Francie told Ronan and his dad. She opened the door and stood up, wincing only slightly from the lingering pain. "Thank you for dinner!" she said before slamming the truck door.

Ronan's dad waited until Sylvie opened the door before pulling the truck out of the driveway.

Francie had never felt so glad to see her grandmother.

"What happened to your foot?" she asked, as Francie hobbled toward the door.

"I don't really know," Francie replied, entering the warm house and easing into a chair at the table by the window. Sylvie walked over to the stove and brought back two cups of chamomile tea and then sat down next to Francie to listen to her tell about her evening.

Chapter 20

The next morning, the bright blue sky offered no hint of the storm the night before. The garden, however, was covered in branches and fallen trees. Francie and Sylvie spent the morning working together to drag them off crushed tomato plants and flowers. Sylvie told Francie to break the smaller branches to put them in the compost pile in the back of the garden. Francie was thankful for the task, which helped keep her mind off of gunshots and mountain lions.

Francie's foot occasionally throbbed as they worked, but the feeling was faint compared to the burning sensation she had felt the night before. There was no outward sign that anything had happened. She had no markings on her foot and it wasn't swollen, but whenever she thought of it an uneasy feeling stirred in her stomach.

As they were heading in for lunch, Sylvie noticed a jagged hole in one of the panes of glass in the greenhouse, and told Francie she'd need to drive forty minutes over to the nearest hardware store to pick up a new pane. Francie decided to stay home and finish reading *Charlie and the Chocolate Factory*, which she'd hardly touched since the first night she had arrived.

Francie watched Sylvie pull out of the driveway and then sat down at the table to read. She found herself unable to focus on the words on the page, her thoughts returning time and time again to the image of the mother and baby mountain lion she had seen at Ronan's house. Had Ronan's dad shot one of them? If he shot the mother, would the baby be okay? She then thought of Augustus, nearly torn apart by a mountain lion, and of the bloody chicken coop Ronan's dad had seen in the storm. Why was she so concerned about such a dangerous beast?

After a while, she gave up on reading her book. She walked over to Sylvie's bookshelf and looked at the books. *Colorado Plants & Wildflowers, Western Herbs, The Illustrated Book of Trees, Colorado Gold Miners: A History.* Remembering the photographs in the Fortune Gold Mining Museum, Francie pulled the last book down from the shelf. The photograph on the cover looked much like the picture of Sylvie's great-grandfather in the museum, but looking closely she saw that it was of a different group of men. She opened the book and a piece of paper fluttered to the floor. Francie leaned over and picked up the weathered piece of paper, folded into a square. She walked over to the table, put down the book and unfolded the paper. Then she took a deep breath. In front of her was a worn, yellowed map. It was professionally printed, with orange contour lines marking the mountains. At the bottom it read "Contour Map of Bald Mountain, 14,032 feet, and Surrounding Area". In black ink, to the west of the mountain, someone had drawn a black circle and written "Wald House."

Jenny - Things have been kind of crazy around here. I found a map though and now I really am going to find the house I told you about. Wish me luck!
XO, Francie

Chapter 21

A week later, Francie, Ronan and Rosie pulled in front of the co-op with an empty backpack. Francie fingered the map in the pocket of her shorts, making sure it hadn't fallen out on the bike ride there.

"I still think there's no way Rosie can do this," Ronan grumbled as Francie hopped off his bike.

"I'm not a baby, Ronan," Rosie retorted, leaning her bike against the store.

"Well, it's the only way we're going to get a chance to go," Francie replied. "Your mom's not going to let you take off for an entire day without her."

"Hey!" Rosie protested, her hands on her hips. "I'm going to to tell mom you guys are being mean to me!"

"Since when are you so into going anyway?" Ronan asked Francie, ignoring his sister. "I thought you had decided you 'didn't want to take any more long hikes anyway.'" He spoke in a poor imitation of Francie's voice.

Francie didn't reply. She knew he was bitter because she hadn't returned his calls or stopped by for nearly a week. After the incident with the mountain lion, she hadn't been eager to return to Ronan's house, though she wasn't even entirely sure why. When she found the map, she felt excited about making another attempt to find the stone house. She had taken it as a sign that she should resume her search. And yet it had taken her a few days to decide whether or not to share the information with Ronan. She knew sharing it with him would mean committing again to a trip to find it and she still felt a knot in her stomach when she thought about Augustus's story. Plus, her foot continued to throb occasionally and she wondered if she could even make it up the trail to the house.

But Francie hadn't been able to stop thinking about the map and what she might find by following it. It had never particularly bothered her before that her mother had never talked about growing up or about her family and that Francie hadn't even known her grandmother before this summer. But it had suddenly become important to her to know more about her family's past. Ultimately she decided that she couldn't resist the thought of discovering the cabin that Sylvie's great-grandfather had lived in so long ago. She kept thinking of the picture of him with his arm around the mountain lion and needed to know more about him.

When Francie, Ronan and Rosie entered the store, Augustus offered his usual greeting. Francie was relieved to see him wearing a flannel again so that she wouldn't have to be further reminded of his story by the sight of his scar.

With six dollars between them, they picked out apples and a small bag of gorp to add to the peanut butter sandwiches Francie had already packed.

"And a huge bag of gummy worms!" Rosie insisted.

"What are you kids up to today?" Augustus asked as Francie placed the food on the counter.

"We're going to find this really cool—" Rosie began.

"Just going down to the creek," Ronan interrupted. "To have a picnic." He shot Rosie a dirty look that Francie hoped Augustus didn't notice.

"Beautiful day for it," he answered.

Francie breathed a sigh of relief when they walked out the door.

- - -

It took them half an hour, with Francie on Rosie's bike and Rosie riding grudgingly on Ronan's seat, to reach the trailhead. When they found it, marked by a wooden sign faded grey with age, they carefully hid their bikes in the bushes and then, after a quick look at the map, headed into the woods. Francie's apprehension all but disappeared as they hiked up the overgrown dirt trail. They were just walking in the woods, as she and Ronan had done so many times before. The woods felt anything but frightening—the air was clean and clear, the birds were singing above them and even the branches snapping under their feet seemed to Francie to be making a cheerful noise. Francie's foot ached a little bit, but not enough to slow her down. Of course, they had to stop every few minutes to convince Rosie to keep up. After the first fifteen minutes, Francie broke into the bag of gummy worms to bribe Rosie. She was worried that at this rate the gummy worms would have Rosie doubled over with a stomach ache before they made it even halfway up the trail, but for now they kept her going.

Between bites of gummy worms, Rosie sang as loudly as she could. Ronan warned her that she was going to use up all of her energy singing, but soon he and Francie joined in. The singing seemed to work even better than the gummy worms had and before they knew it, they could hear the sound of rushing water. As they walked closer to the sound, the air felt cooler on their bare arms and legs. Soon they were looking down at a waterfall, marking the halfway point up the trail.

"I don't think I've ever seen a real waterfall before," Francie exclaimed.

"Only fake ones?" Ronan joked.

"Yeah. I'm serious. I mean, I know someone who has one going into her pool, but it's not for real like this one."

"What are we waiting for?" Rosie asked. "Isn't this where we are eating lunch?"

"How can you even be hungry after all those gummy worms?" Ronan scoffed, but he headed off the trail toward the water.

They ate lunch on a rock near the waterfall. A light mist of water cooled them off as they ate.

After lunch, Francie was eager to start hiking again so that they could get to the house and home in time not to arouse suspicion from Ronan's parents. He had told them he was taking Rosie hiking, but Francie was pretty sure they weren't imagining that meant he was taking her three miles into the woods on a trail that Augustus had warned them against. But Ronan insisted that he show her something first.

"You never know when you'll get a chance to be near a real live waterfall again," he said, showing his crooked smile.

Ronan instructed Rosie, who was using the empty gummy bear bag to catch minnows in a small pool of water, to wait for them for a minute.

"Stop acting like I'm a baby, Ronan!" she whined, glaring up at him. But she remained by the pool, focused on catching more fish.

Francie followed as Ronan scrambled over rocks next to the water. As they neared the waterfall, the cool water splashing at her gave her goose bumps. Soon they stood nearly next to the waterfall, holding onto the wet rock wall with their hands and trying to maintain their balances on the increasingly slippery rock beneath them.

"Okay, now hold your breath and follow me," Ronan called to her over the roar of water. Taking a step, he disappeared behind the watery curtain. Francie braced herself for the cold and, closing her eyes, took a large step, her foot sliding slightly on the rock. When she opened her eyes, it took a minute for them to adjust and for her to see Ronan in the darkened cave.

"We're behind the waterfall!" she yelled, laughing.

"Yup. The for real waterfall!" Ronan yelled back.

Francie pressed against the cave wall, shivering slightly, amazed at the power of the water rushing before her. She looked at Ronan. He smiled at her. A rainbow, made by the sun and water, danced above him on the cave wall.

After a minute, Ronan nodded to the left to indicate that they should head back out. Once again, Francie took a deep breath and stepped through the water. When she opened her eyes, she saw Rosie standing on the rock, her arms folded across her chest.

"You guys didn't tell me you were going to take forever in there," she said indignantly, when Francie and Ronan reached her.

"Sorry Rosie," Francie said. "But did you catch any minnows?"

"The stupid bag ripped and they all swam away," she replied. "Can we go already?"

Francie grabbed the backpack and they climbed back up to the trail. As they continued up the second half of the trail, they found it less marked. Several times they had to stop and once they even walked five minutes out of the way before realizing they had taken a wrong turn. The lack of gummy worms wasn't helping either and finally Rosie, tired of them ignoring her complaints, sat down on the trail and refused to take a step further.

"Fine Rosie. Then we'll leave you here and you can get eaten by mountain lions and bears," Ronan said.

Francie opened her map and showed Rosie how close they were. "Please Rosie. You know, that house belonged to gold miners. And if there's any gold in there, I promise you can have it." Francie looked at Rosie, who looked genuinely tired, and wondered if maybe it was a bad idea after all to have dragged her all the way up there. But they were so close.

"What do you think you'd do with a house full of gold, Rosie?" she asked and was surprised when Rosie perked up and began talking about how she'd use the gold to buy ponies and pay for riding lessons. By the time Rosie was on her twelfth horse (a pinto named Princess who liked to eat flowers), they reached what looked like the end of the trail. In front of them, huge grey boulders blocked the way. They looked as if they'd dropped out of the sky simply to prevent them from reaching their destination.

"Okay Francie. This sucks. We definitely made a wrong turn," Ronan said.

Augustus's voice echoed in Francie's head: *But then I came to a point where I was surrounded by huge boulders...*

"No," she replied. "We definitely didn't."

"What—"

"This is right. I know this is right." She looked up. "But I can't imagine how we're going to get up there."

"Well, if you say so. Okay, you guys wait down here and I'll give it a try," Ronan said.

"No way!" Rosie cried. "You left me out last time at the waterfall. I get to go first this time."

"I don't think that's such a good idea…" Francie began. She was suddenly filled with panic at the idea that she had dragged Rosie and Ronan up here. Up here where Augustus had been nearly killed by a mountain lion; where Augustus had specifically warned them not to go; where no one would ever find them if they never came back because no one knew where they had gone. But Rosie had already begun to climb. Francie and Ronan watched as Rosie scrambled up the rock.

"How'd you learn how to climb so good?" Ronan asked, looking up.

"I can do lots of things you don't know about," Rosie said, looking down. She stuck out her tongue but then smiled.

"Don't look so worried, Francie," Ronan said to her. "We're almost there. House full of gold, right?" He smiled at her and reached up to begin climbing the rock.

Francie looked up at Rosie again and noticed her reaching up to grab onto a thin sapling growing out of a crack in the rock.

"Rosie!" she yelled, but it was too late. She watched in horror as Rosie grabbed on, pulling the sapling out of the rock and losing her balance. Even as Rosie tumbled backward, bouncing of the rock and landing on top of Ronan, Francie kept thinking, this isn't happening, this isn't happening, this isn't happening.

Chapter 22

After the eerie thud of Rosie's fall, the forest itself seemed to hold its breath. Francie looked at Rosie, her body twisted unnaturally on the ground, her white blonde hair covering her face, a pool of blood forming next to her head. Ronan had pulled himself out from under her and was leaning over her, grabbing his own arm at the same time. Francie could see him, could see his mouth moving, could see tears wetting his freckled cheeks, but she couldn't move. Ronan stood up and, with one arm, began to shake Francie.

"Francie! Snap out of it! Francie, please! I need you here, Francie! Wake up!" She nodded silently and then leaned down, next to Rosie. She thought of the robin and of her grandmother gently feeling for a heartbeat. She put her ear over Rosie's heart and sighed with relief at the familiar sound of life. She moved Rosie's hair from her face and gasped at the sight of her bloodied nose and mouth. But she leaned over and felt the warm air of her breath.

"She's alive," she whispered to Ronan. He let out a sob.

"We need to get her home," she said. Ronan nodded, and attempted to pull off his t-shirt. He didn't move his left arm and winced in pain when he pulled his t-shirt over it. With his right arm, he held his shirt against the back of Rosie's head. Francie was reminded of their afternoon in the museum, which suddenly seemed like ages ago. It occurred to her that if they had never broken into the museum, they would never have found themselves looking for a house they saw in a picture.

"Are you okay?" Francie asked.

"I'm fine," Ronan grunted, his expression showing otherwise.

"Seriously Ronan, just at least tell me what's going on so we can figure out how to help Rosie."

"I am going to get Rosie down this mountain," he said through his teeth. "It's just, it's nothing, but when she fell, my arm—" he cut himself off, staring at something behind Francie. Francie turned to follow his gaze. The mountain lion stood on a small boulder behind her.

"We've got to grab Rosie, we've got to run!" Ronan yelled.

"No," Francie said.

"What are you talking about, Francie? Have you lost your mind? The mountain lion smelled Rosie's blood!" Ronan was frantically attempting to pick up Rosie with his right arm.

Francie stood up. The mountain lion took a step forward.

"Please trust me, Ronan," Francie said. "I know it doesn't make a lot of sense but she's not here for the smell of blood. I think…I think she's here because she smelled me…I know this mountain lion…and I think she might be able to help us."

Francie took a step forward. She could hear her grandmother as if she were right there beside her. "You have a gift, Francie," she said to her. She looked at the mountain lion and realized that she didn't have a choice. She had to let herself believe that it was true. And suddenly, she knew it as much as she'd ever known anything before. She looked at the mountain lion's yellow eyes and felt the familiar energy pulse through her. This time, instead of shaking, she took a step toward the mountain lion and reached out her arm, holding out her palm. The lion took another step forward and then leapt from the rock, landing a few feet from where Francie stood. She walked toward Francie and then nuzzled her face against Francie's hand.

Francie leaned down and scratched the coarse fur between her ears. She looked at her golden eyes.

"It isn't so much that I didn't trust you," Francie whispered to her. "It's just that I didn't trust me." She turned back and looked at Ronan, who was staring at her with his mouth open. Then she let out a yelp of joy, for Rosie too was staring at her in disbelief.

"You're awake, Rosie!" she cried.

"No. I'm definitely dreaming," Rosie said, sitting up and wiping blood from her nose with the back of her hand, but continuing to stare. Francie threw her arms around the mountain lion. She was surprised for a moment at the coarseness of her fur, but she leaned her head against her and was comforted by her warmth. She whispered, "Please help us." She lay against her for another minute and then stood up.

"Rosie?" Francie asked, "Where are you hurt?"

Rosie wiped her nose again and then looked at the blood on the back of her hand.

"My nose, my head, my leg." She began to cry. "And all over. I hurt all over. I want to go home."

"It's okay, Rosie, we're going to get you home. I promise you. You're going to have to trust me though, okay?"

"Okay," Rosie whimpered.

"And you're going to have a great story to tell, Rosie," Francie said, trying to smile. "Because what I need you to do is to grab onto the back of this mountain lion."

"Francie!" Ronan protested. "I have no idea what's going on with you, but there's no way I'm letting you put my sister on that lion."

"We have to, Ronan," Francie replied. "What else are we going to do? You're going to carry her down with a broken arm? I'm going to carry her down by myself? I could try but it would take forever. Please, Ronan. We'll be right next to her. I promise you, it'll be okay."

"No way, Francie. No way." Ronan leaned down again to pick up Rosie.

"Ronan, it's okay," Rosie said. "I think we should try it."

The mountain lion stood next to Francie silently.

"I need your help," Francie said to Ronan, as she leaned down to pick up Rosie. Ronan kneeled down, shaking his head. But, with his right arm, he helped lift Rosie up and onto her left leg. Her right foot seemed to hang at an odd angle and she cried out in pain as they helped her up.

"Are you okay?" Ronan asked her.

"Mmmhmmm," Rosie moaned.

"You're being super brave," Francie told her.

The mountain lion took a step toward Rosie and stood in front of her, as if she already understood the plan. Rosie leaned down and grabbed onto her neck. She gingerly pulled her right leg over the mountain lion, whimpering slightly as she did so. The mountain lion staggered momentarily under Rosie's weight and then stood firmly. The t-shirt had fallen off Rosie's head as she stood up and Ronan grabbed it and held it against the back of Rosie's head. It was soaked in blood, but the trickle of blood seemed to have slowed down.

"This is even better than a horse," Rosie said, managing a small smile. "She's scratchy though." She adjusted herself against the rough fur.

"Let's walk as fast as we can," Francie said, and took a step, hoping that the mountain lion would understand. She looked up at Francie and then followed, her breath labored, with Rosie clinging to her neck and Ronan walking next to her, keeping his t-shirt in place on Rosie's cut. As they walked, Rosie began to get drowsy and to nod off.

"Stay awake, Rosie!" Ronan kept yelling, shaking her slightly.

"Maybe you could tell us more about your ponies," Francie suggested.

"I'm too tired. Can you tell me, Francie? What would you do with all the gold?"

"Hmmm. That's a good question." Francie thought about it. "I really don't know."

Rosie looked disappointed with her answer.

"But I think I'd buy some horses for you, Rosie," Francie said quickly. She thought back to the My Little Pony collection she had when she was Rosie's age and began to tell Rosie about the magical horses that she would buy for her.

And so, with Ronan holding his t-shirt to Rosie's head, Rosie clinging to the mountain lion, and Francie telling stories, they made their way slowly down the mountain.

When they had almost reached the road, the mountain lion came to an abrupt stop. Francie tried to encourage her to continue, but she wouldn't move.

"We can find someone to help us," Ronan said, squinting up at the late afternoon sky. "Loggers start coming home along the road this time of day."

Francie nodded and she and Ronan gently lifted Rosie off the mountain lion. Francie knelt down, looking into the lion's golden eyes again.

"Thank you," she said. She hugged her, and noticed that the lion's back was warm and wet with Rosie's blood. She stood up and the mountain lion turned from her and ran, quickly disappearing into the woods.

Ronan and Francie looked at each other. His eyes were full of questions, but he didn't say a word.

"Let's get Rosie home," he said. They lifted her up and carried her to the side of the road. Within minutes, a dirty blue truck pulled up next to them. Ronan recognized the driver, a thick-necked man with wide smile, as a friend of his dad's. His smile disappeared immediately when he saw the dried blood smeared across Rosie's face. He let out a low whistle.

"What on earth have you kids been doing?" he asked. But he

helped them load the bikes and Rosie into the truck without any further questions.

"I'm taking you kids straight to the hospital," he told them, speeding down the dirt road, doing his best to avoid the potholes. "We'll call your dad from there."

"I guess you're going to get in big trouble Ronan," Rosie said, letting out a small laugh.

"You know what, Rosie? I'm glad you still have your sense of humor, even after a day like today," Ronan replied.

Francie looked at him and could almost see the tension flowing from his body. They were on their way to the hospital. Rosie was going to be okay. She leaned back into the sticky vinyl seat and closed her eyes. *Thank you*, she thought, *thank you*, over and over again.

Chapter 23

The hour Francie spent in the hospital before her grandmother arrived felt as surreal as Rosie's fall. Looking back, it would be hard for her to imagine that it wasn't actually a dream—the blinding florescent lights; the doctors wheeling Rosie away; the hard plastic chairs she and Ronan sat on while he waited for x-rays. Then suddenly Ronan's parents were rushing in, his mom hugging Ronan so hard that he yelped in pain and his dad yelling at him until the doctor came out and told them that, a set leg and twenty-three stitches later, Rosie was going to be okay, at which point his dad told Ronan over and over again how he was just glad they all made it home. The doctor then summoned Ronan and his parents in so that she could show them the x-rays and put his arm in a cast. Francie sat in the waiting room alone, the images from the afternoon playing over and over again in her mind.

When her grandmother showed up in her faded brown dress, smelling of the garden and of sunlight, Francie had never been so glad to see anyone in her life.

"I'm sorry," Francie whispered, when her grandmother greeted her with a hug.

"Shh," she soothed her. "Let's get you home."

When they got home, Sylvie immediately went into the bathroom and ran a warm, lavender bath for Francie. When Francie dried off and dressed in a t-shirt and sweat pants, the hospital felt worlds away. Her grandmother waited at the kitchen table with two steaming cups of tea.

Francie sat down and looked at the tea, but didn't pick it up.

"I found your map," Francie whispered into her tea.

"I know," her grandmother replied. Francie looked up in surprise.

"I'm sorry," she said, fighting back tears. "I should never have taken the map and I should never ever have brought Rosie into those woods. Augustus even told me not to go there and I went anyway and now Rosie…" Francie stopped, her throat too thick to speak. Her grandmother reached her hand over the table and placed it on top of Francie's. Francie could see the dirt from the garden under her grandmother's fingernails. Her hand felt warm, as it had on the day she had saved the robin.

"Rosie is going to be just fine," her grandmother said to her. She sighed. "That doesn't mean you should've brought Rosie up there, but I don't think you need me to tell you that now. What exactly did Augustus tell you about those woods?"

"He told me that there were mountain lions there and that it was dangerous. Except, you know what? The mountain lion actually saved Rosie. She helped us carry her down the mountain." Francie looked up. Her grandmother was looking at her intently and Francie noticed for the first time that they shared the same earth-brown eyes.

"You used your gift," her grandmother said softly.

"Yes," she said.

"You are a very special girl, Francie. You really are."

"Thank you," Francie whispered. She looked in the window at their reflection—a granddaughter and grandmother, sitting at the table drinking tea together.

"I'm glad I came here this summer," Francie said.

"I am too."

Chapter 24

When Francie awoke to a dark room and her grandmother's snoring, she felt disoriented and couldn't at first figure out what had pulled her from such a deep slumber. Then she heard a scratching noise at the door. She waited, but it didn't go away. Her grandmother continued to snore and Francie debated waking her, but instead stood up and walked quietly over to the kitchen window. She pressed her face against the glass and peered into the darkness. Her breath caught at the sight of the mountain lion standing outside the door. For a brief instant, fear pulsed through her body. Then she thought of Rosie and opened the door as quietly as she could, never having noticed before how much it creaked.

Outside, the cold air startled her awake. She kneeled down to face the mountain lion.

"Hello," she said. Francie could still see the dark stain of Rosie's blood on her back. The mountain lion rubbed against her but soon pulled away and began to walk toward the garden. Francie watched her as the mountain lion ran back to her and then walked away again. Francie took a deep breath and followed her. She was surprised at how well she could see with only the moonlight to guide her. As she followed the mountain lion by the outhouse, she remembered her first night at her grandmother's, when she had followed her mother on the same trail. How scared she had been then of just being outside!

At the edge of the garden, right where it met the woods, the mountain lion stopped. She walked over to a pine with low-hanging branches and disappeared behind them. Francie ducked under the branches to follow her. Something moved next to the tree. As her eyes adjusted to the darkness in the shadows, Francie recognized the cub. He lay on his side and whole body shook violently as if with cold, though the night air was mild. The mountain lion walked over and sat next to him.

"What's wrong?" Francie asked. The mountain lion just looked at her. Francie knelt down and looked at the cub's face. His tongue hung out and his eyes rolled back in his head. His breath was loud and jagged.

"Oh no, what's happened to you?" Francie looked over the cub's body and noticed a dark stain covering his right front paw. The paw was swollen to nearly twice its normal size. Francie began to cry, her hands covering her face.

The mountain lion nudged her with her nose, almost knocking her over. Francie looked up.

"I know you need help," she said, wiping her eyes with the back of her hand. "I think I can help you, but I need my grandmother. Stay here, just stay here and I'll be right back." She stood up and ran toward the house. At the side window, where the robin had crashed weeks ago, Francie banged her fists against the glass.

Her grandmother opened the window, her long grey hair wild from sleep.

"Francie? What is it?"

"The mountain lion," Francie sobbed. "Her baby is hurt!"

Her grandmother turned from the window and appeared a minute later in the garden, barefoot in her flannel pajamas, her hair still in wild tangles. The golden locket around her neck shone in the moonlight.

"Where are they?" she asked. Francie ran ahead through the garden and her grandmother followed.

116

When Francie pulled aside the branches of the tree, she saw that the cub lay on the ground by himself.

"They were both here," Francie said, looking around.

"His mother will be back when it's time," her grandmother said. She leaned down and inspected the cub's paw.

"A bullet," she spat out the words. "You can see here where it went right through."

Francie looked at the paw again. "In the hailstorm," she said slowly. "When I was at Ronan's, the night when my foot…"

They looked at each other.

Sylvie held the injured paw in one hand and placed the other hand gently on top of it. When she removed her hand, the cub's paw looked considerably less swollen.

"Let's get him inside," Sylvie said.

The cub whimpered as they lifted him up. Francie staggered slightly under his weight.

"Let me know if you need to rest and put him down."

"I'm okay," Francie replied, as they made their way slowly across the garden.

Once in the house, Francie pulled the quilt off of her bed and made a bed on the floor for the cub. Sylvie turned on the light and inspected the cub's foot more thoroughly.

"It looks like the bullet went all the way through, so at least we won't have to torture the poor thing with pulling it out," she murmured. "It's terribly infected though." She walked over to the kitchen and began pulling jars off of the shelf and heating up water. Francie sat next to the cub and stroked his back. Sylvie returned with a jar of clear liquid and another full of thick paste and a brush. She lifted the cub's head and poured the clear liquid down his throat. The cub stirred, gagging slightly, but then swallowed obediently before falling back asleep. Sylvie pulled the brush out of the other jar and lightly brushed it over the cub's paw. The cub flinched and pulled his paw away, but didn't make a sound. Sylvie waited until he lay his paw back down, applied more paste and then sat down in front of the cub.

"Should we bandage it?" Francie asked.

"We'll need to watch him, but as long as he doesn't lick it, the air will help dry out the infection."

"Is he going to be okay?"

"Yes. He'll need to rest here for a couple of days, but I think he should be fine." They both looked at the cub, who had fallen asleep between them. "We should probably get back to sleep, don't you think?"

Francie nodded, though she no longer felt tired. Minutes later her grandmother, who never seemed to have any trouble falling right to sleep, was snoring again. Francie rolled over on her side and looked at the cub sleeping on the floor next to her bed. She sat up, quietly pulled another blanket off of her bed and lay down next to the cub. The cub's fur was softer than his mother's fur, but still scratchy, as Rosie had described it. He wheezed lightly in his sleep. Francie put her arm around him and soon drifted off to sleep as well.

Chapter 25

The next morning, Francie opened the door to use the outhouse and found a dead rabbit on the doorstep. She was about to scream when Sylvie walked up behind her and stood next to her in the doorway.

"I was just wondering what we were going to do about breakfast for the cub. Looks like his mom has already taken care of it." She looked down at the rabbit. "I think we'll let him eat his breakfast outside though."

Francie looked in at the cub, who had lifted his head and was staring at Francie and Sylvie.

"He looks a lot better already," she remarked. The cub struggled to his feet and limped slowly over to the door. Francie and Sylvie backed away and watched him lie down next to the rabbit. Immediately, he began to tear it apart with his teeth.

"Do you want some tea and oatmeal?" Sylvie asked.

"I think I just lost my appetite," Francie replied.

After eating most of the rabbit and drinking from a bowl that Francie set out for him, the cub limped back to the quilt and fell back asleep. This time, Francie helped Sylvie apply the paste to his foot. He flinched slightly in his sleep but otherwise didn't move.

"Shouldn't he be awake now?" Francie asked.

"Actually, he should be asleep. They are usually crepuscular, awake in the evening and early morning. It's unusual that you have seen her mother in the daylight so often. She must have been really drawn to you."

"But the cub slept all night too."

"Well, he's still healing," Sylvie replied. "And don't forget that Ronan and Rosie are healing too. Why don't you pick some flowers and I'll drive you down there to check on how they're doing?"

Francie walked around the garden slowly, clipping daisies, red echinacea flowers and yellow agastache, taking her time with each one. She was nervous about going to Ronan's house. She was scared to see his dad, who had been so angry at the hospital and worried about the condition Rosie might be in. Mostly, though, she didn't want to see Ronan. It was one thing to make fish flip out of the water. It was quite another to call over a wild mountain lion and ask her to give your friend's sister a ride.

When Francie's fingers strained to fit around the bouquet, she realized she couldn't put it off any longer. She brought the flowers inside, where Sylvie tied them with yarn and stuck them in a mason jar. They both admired the flowers on the table.

"You should sell flowers at the co-op too," Francie said.

"Not a bad idea," Sylvie replied. "Especially when I have such a good bouquet maker around. Well, around for a couple more weeks at least." She turned the bouquet around to inspect it from all sides. "Seventeen more days to be exact," she said, more to herself than to Francie.

Francie was startled at the mention of her time left in Fortune. When her mother had first mentioned that she would be spending the entire summer at her grandmother's, it had stretched before her, an endless amount of time. Now, suddenly, she could see the end and didn't even know if she wanted it to arrive.

"Well, anyway," Sylvie said quickly, "Let's get going to Ronan's house."

Chapter 26

Ronan opened the door when they pulled into the driveway. He stood in the doorway, squinting in the sunlight, wearing his usual jeans and faded t-shirt, and offering Francie his usual crooked smile. The only difference was a bright blue cast on his left arm.

"I can't leave the cub at home too long," Sylvie said. "But I'll be back in an hour to pick you up." Francie nodded and hopped out of the car.

"Where is everyone?" Francie asked Ronan, suddenly noticing the empty driveway.

"My mom stayed overnight at the hospital with Rosie and my dad just went over there to pick them up and bring them home. They had to watch her overnight in case of a concussion or something like that."

"Oh." She held out the flowers. "I brought some flowers."

"Gee thanks, I just love flowers," Ronan joked.

"Well, they aren't for you anyway. Can you put them inside?" she handed him the bouquet.

"Sure," he replied, disappearing into the house. Francie wasn't sure whether or not to follow and instead sat down on the front steps. A minute later, Ronan came out with two popsicles in his right hand.

"Thanks," she said and they sat next to each other on the steps.

"So," Ronan said after a while. "I guess we'll probably never get to the stone house."

"No, I guess not." Francie wiped purple popsicle juice off her knee.

"You know, I never thought a girl who didn't know how to ride bike would know how to tame a mountain lion."

"Me neither," she said. "Really, I promise that I didn't either."

"You're a strange girl, you know that?" She looked over at him and was once again relieved by his crooked smile.

"Maybe I am," she said, and laughed, because they were sitting in the sun and eating popsicles and because suddenly everything felt right.

Chapter 27

The cub seemed to be waiting for Francie when she got home. He sat up on his quilt, his injured front paw elevated, and watched her walk in.

"He's looking so much better," Francie said, walking over to sit next to him. The cub lay his head on Francie's lap.

"It's like he's a pet dog or something," Francie laughed.

"Yes," said Sylvie, looking at the two of them. "But don't forget that in a couple of days he'll go back to his mother."

- - -

Four days later when the mountain lion came to get her cub with a scratch at the door sometime near dawn, Francie let out a small cry of protest. She had been sleeping soundly next to the cub, and was already used to his warm body and sweet, wild scent. Francie's cry woke Sylvie from her sleep. She sat up in bed and sighed.

"I'm sorry, Francie, but we knew it would happen."

The cub rushed to the door and began scratching as well.

"Hold on, hold on. You two are going to break down my door," Sylvie admonished. Sure enough, Francie could see scratches in the wood, even in the dim room.

Sylvie opened the door.

"Wait," Francie cried, jumping up. The cub paused and she threw her arms around him one last time. The cub nuzzled his head into Francie's neck and then took a step away. The mountain lion looked at them with her golden eyes.

"I'll miss you," Francie said to both of them. The cub rubbed up against his mother. Then, the two of them turned and bounded toward the forest, the cub limping only slightly.

Francie and Sylvie stood looking at the forest and the still black sky.

"I think going back to bed is out of the question, don't you?" Sylvie asked. Francie nodded.

"I have an idea," she said. "Let's get some breakfast because we're going to need some energy. Do you want to pick some tomatoes and I can make us omelets?"

"I've never picked tomatoes in the dark before," Francie replied. She grabbed a basket and walked to the garden. She paused for a moment before picking the tomatoes. The flowers and plants in the garden shone silvery blue in the moonlight. She felt pride pulse through her as she looked around and realized that she had helped create such a magical place. As she picked the tomatoes, the eastern sky began to lighten. She walked back in with a basket full of tomatoes, wondering what her grandmother had in mind for the day.

An hour later, Francie found herself in the passenger seat of her grandmother's car, bouncing along the dirt road. Her grandmother had mentioned nothing more than a hike, so she was surprised when she pulled up alongside the faded wood sign.

"But this is where..." Francie began, her voice trailing off.

"How do you feel about going to the stone house together?" Sylvie asked, turning to her and studying her face.

Francie took a deep breath and then nodded.

As they started up the trail, Francie was happy to simply follow her grandmother. She wouldn't have to find the way this time. She thought about trying to coax Rosie up the trail. This time, she tried to keep up with her grandmother who, even with her long gray braid and wrinkled skin, hiked at a brisk clip.

"I hope I'm in as good of shape as you are when I'm old," she gasped when they stopped for a water break.

"Who says I'm old?" Sylvie replied, smiling.

Soon they had passed the waterfall and, just as they were getting ready to stop for lunch, Francie could see the boulders in the distance. Before they reached them, her grandmother suddenly veered off the trail.

"Where are we going?" Francie asked.

"To the house," her grandmother responded.

Francie stopped and pointed.

"But I thought the boulders...Augustus had mentioned you have to pass the boulders."

Sylvie stopped and looked closely at Francie.

"Did he mention that he was lost when he was on them?"

"I don't remember," she replied.

"Well, he was. And he should never have come up here by himself," Sylvie snapped.

"Are you still mad at him about it?" Francie asked.

"Well, I don't suppose I'm mad but..."

"Because Augustus thinks you're mad at him is all. You think he thinks you're a witch and he thinks you're mad at him but I think you're both wrong." Francie surprised herself with her own boldness, but Sylvie looked thoughtful in response.

"Perhaps you're right," she said. Then she turned around and didn't say anything for the rest of the hike.

As Francie followed her grandmother, she realized that she could never have found the stone house on her own. Her grandmother walked through the woods confidently, but followed no markings or trails that Francie could see. After a while, the terrain became steeper and, just as Francie was about to ask that they stop for a rest, they came to a clearing in the woods. Francie looked up and, perched on a rock, stood the stone house. Time had left its mark. The house no longer had a chimney and ivy wound its way over most of the roof. Still, Francie felt like she was stepping into a scene from the past.

Sylvie turned to her and smiled.

"Here it is," she said. They began to walk up the crumbling stone steps. Francie stood for a minute in front of the house and thought of the photograph of her relatives, standing right where she stood now.

"Should we go in?" Sylvie asked.

When Francie reached to open the door, she realized it was missing a doorknob and most of the red paint had chipped away over time. The bottom half of the door was marked with deep, jagged, vertical grooves. She bent down and ran her finger down one of them, thinking of the cub clawing at Sylvie's door to get to his mother. When she stood up and pushed open the door, a chipmunk stared at her from a packed dirt floor and then climbed up the wall and out the window. It was dark and cool inside with no furniture or artwork left behind by her relatives. Francie remembered telling Rosie about a house full of gold. She wasn't sure what she had actually expected, but she felt momentarily disappointed.

Sylvie walked back outside. "Here, sit down next to me!" she called to Francie. Francie followed her and sat next to her on a stone bench under one of the windows. They looked out at an evergreen-covered mountain in front of them and then endless white-capped mountains beyond. The sun felt warm on Francie's face.

"So this is where my great-great-great-grandfather lived," Francie said, counting the "greats" on her fingertips. She leaned back against the wall.

Sylvie pointed in front of them. "That wall over there is where he used to crack walnuts with me when I was little."

"Maybe the chipmunk we saw in the house is the great-granddaughter of the ones you saw with him," Francie mused, smiling at the thought.

Sylvie laughed. "Could be."

They sat quietly for a moment.

"Well, I guess they had a nice view," Francie said after a while.

Sylvie nodded. "I love coming up here and looking out at the mountains. I've always found it calming."

"I never even thought about how I had a great-great-great-grandpa or where he came from before I came here," Francie said, running her hand along the rough stone of the bench. "I guess I didn't even think that much about how I had a grandma either."

Sylvie closed her eyes and leaned her head back against the stone wall. "You know, I love your mother very much," she said. "I wish that we were closer and I promise to work on that. I think it was hard for her, growing up here and having her dad leave like that."

"Why did he leave?"

"Well, Francie, you know how I told you how some people may not really…appreciate your special connection with animals?"

"Yeah."

"I could never really quite believe your grandfather stayed in Fortune, to tell you the truth. But we were young and I suppose in love and he decided to stay. And it was fine at first. He certainly kept himself busy, opening this store and that. You know, before he arrived, Fortune was just some boarded up buildings. And when your mother came along we were happy for a while. I think he must have had some idea that I had an unusual relationship with animals, but then one morning he found me out in the garden with your mother and a young black bear. Your mother was petting the bear and laughing. Her father asked what was going on, and I tried to explain, but oh, that spooked him. He didn't like it one bit. I told him not to worry about it of course. But little by little he began to notice my way with animals more and more. There were the snakes in the front yard and the mountain lions of course. I think he had decided already that he didn't like the way his life had turned out—a big city boy living in this small town. And then it turns out his wife has these strange tendencies…and so he left. And he never came back."

"Did my mother ever see him again?"

"Not that I know of."

"My father left too," Francie said. "But he moved right up the street so it's not really the same." Francie felt sad for the little girl that her mother had been.

"Does my mother have the same gift?" she asked, turning to Sylvie.

"I don't know, Francie. You have to both want to have it and to believe that you do or else it isn't going to mean anything. After her father left, your mother was never interested in finding out."

Francie looked out over the mountains. "Sometimes I think that I want to just stay here."

Sylvie shook her head. "I love having you here, Francie. And I wish that we didn't live so far away. But I know what it feels like to lose a daughter. Your mother might not see things the way you do all the time, but she loves you very much."

They were both quiet.

"Maybe you could come back next summer, though," Sylvie offered.

"That would be nice." Francie sighed. "But next summer seems like a long time from now."

Sylvie reached up and unclasped the necklace from her neck.

"This was my great-grandmother's, and I'd like you to have it," she said, handing it to Francie.

"It's beautiful." Francie looked at the locket in her hand. "I didn't know that it was hers."

"I like to imagine that my great-grandfather found the gold to make this necklace, but I'm not really sure," Sylvie said.

Francie opened the locket and saw that it held two black-and-white photographs. She recognized her relatives immediately. One was of Sylvie's great-grandmother, whose high cheekbones and light hair reminded Francie once again of her mother. The other was of Sylvie's great-grandfather, who seemed to be looking at something beyond the camera.

"Thank you," Francie said.

"I figured this was a good place to give that to you."

Francie looked at the photographs again and then closed the locket. She asked Sylvie to help clasp the gold chain.

"It looks nice against the blue beads in your other necklace," Sylvie said. Francie looked down at the necklace that Jenny had given her as a going away gift and immediately felt better about going home, thinking that soon she would see Jenny again.

When they made their way down the steps to return to Sylvie's, Francie turned to take one last look at the stone house. She smiled and rubbed her locket with her hands, feeling as if she were bringing part of the house back with her.

Chapter 28

When they pulled into Sylvie's driveway, Francie was surprised to see a dented green truck in front of the house. It took her a minute to place it as the truck she usually saw parked in front of the co-op.

"What on earth…" Sylvie muttered as she stepped out of the car.

Augustus opened the door of his truck and stepped out.

"Sylvie, Francie," he said, touching the brim of his hat. "I'm real sorry to just drop in unannounced like this. But I have something for Francie and I just couldn't wait."

He grinned at Francie and then walked over to the back of the truck. He opened the hatch and lifted out a turquoise mountain bike with thick black wheels.

"I ordered it a couple weeks ago, when Ronan and Rosie were gone. I knew you wouldn't have a bike again when they came back. I guess now Rosie probably won't be riding hers for a while, but I still thought you might like…"

"Thank you!" Francie interrupted. She ran over and gave Augustus a hug. He stood awkwardly for a moment and then patted her on the back.

"I'm glad you like it, Francie," he said.

"Oh, Augustus, you really shouldn't have," Sylvie was saying, as Francie flung her leg over the seat and began to pedal in circles in the driveway.

"I love it!" she cried. She stopped pedaling and looked from Augustus to Sylvie.

"I probably should have asked you first," Augustus said, turning toward Sylvie.

"No, no, it was kind of you," Sylvie replied. "You certainly meant well. It was too kind though, I shouldn't let you give her something like this." She looked at Francie.

"Can I please keep it?" Francie asked.

"Well, Augustus, clearly you knew exactly what she wanted... Oh, alright, I suppose it's fine with me."

"Thank you!" Francie yelled.

"I'm glad you like it," Augustus repeated, smiling. He paused for a moment, as if he meant to say more. "I guess I should get going," he said finally.

"Well, you ought to at least come in for a cup of tea," Sylvie said.

Augustus raised his eyebrows. "If that's alright..."

"It's alright with me. Francie, come on in and have some tea with us."

"Would it be alright if I just tried out my new bike first?" Francie asked. "I mean, beyond just circles in the driveway. I'd like to take it to show Ronan and Rosie." Sylvie nodded and before she could respond further, Francie took off, pedaling as fast as she could down the road, loving the wind in her face. She laughed out loud, remembering herself only a couple of months ago, slamming her legs into the pedals as Ronan taught her how to ride.

By the time Francie returned to Sylvie's, the trees cast late afternoon shadows over the driveway. She was surprised once again to see Augustus's truck there. Over an hour had passed, and he had stayed. She leaned her bike against the house and opened the front door to find Augustus and Sylvie sitting at the table, talking over empty mugs of tea. They both looked up when she walked in the door.

"Come join us," Sylvie invited, pulling back an empty chair.

"I'll heat up some more tea," Francie replied, before sitting down. She refilled their mugs and then sat down, telling them about her bike ride and about how much better Rosie was feeling. Her head was healing well and she would be in a walking cast in another week. For now, though, she was taking full advantage of her parents' orders that Ronan cater to everything she needed, which was of course driving Ronan crazy.

Augustus ended up staying for dinner. When Sylvie asked him to stay, Francie ran out to pick some tomatoes, basil and rosemary from the garden before Sylvie could change her mind. When she brought them in, Augustus shooed Francie and Sylvie out of the kitchen, insisting that he could make the best pasta sauce they'd ever tasted. As a delicious smell began to fill the house, Sylvie pulled out a faded blue tablecloth and even placed beeswax candles on the table. Francie set the forks and knives on cloth napkins.

"I feel like we're celebrating something," Francie said.

"I think we are," Augustus replied from the kitchen.

"Yes," Sylvie concurred, "I think we are too."

When they sat down to eat, Francie and Sylvie had to agree that the pasta sauce was delicious.

"Well, you both grew the ingredients so I can't take all the credit," Augustus insisted." He patted his stomach. "But I have to admit that I do make a darn good pasta sauce." They all laughed.

When he stood to leave for the evening, Francie thanked him again for her bike.

"No," he said seriously, putting his hand on her shoulder. "Thank you, Francie." He looked behind her at Sylvie and smiled.

That night, Francie wrote her last postcard to Jenny from Fortune. Augustus had printed up new postcards using the photograph of Bald Mountain.

Dear Jenny, I might even see you before this postcard arrives. I have so much to tell you and so much of it takes place right on this mountain in the picture. I can't believe school starts in two weeks! XO, Francie

Chapter 29

Ronan rode his bike up to Sylvie's on Francie's last day in Fortune.

"I got the whole day off from serving Rosie," he said as he circled the driveway on his bike, one hand on the handlebar and the other still in a cast. "It's a good thing too because being laid up with a broken leg has turned her into a monster."

Francie laughed. "I can't really see Rosie as a monster."

"Try making her lemonade. She made me make three different glasses of it because she said each one tasted 'icky'."

Francie began to ride her bike in circles as well.

"What should we do today?" she asked.

"Before we go do something and I forget," Ronan said, "I have something for you." He stopped his bike and dug into his pocket. "I got it at the gem store and I thought you'd like it."

He opened his hand and Francie rode over.

"What is it?" she asked, taking the cone-shaped piece of glass from his hand.

"It's a prism. Hold it up to the sun and it makes rainbows." His face flushed. "Anyway, just thought you might like it," he said, putting his feet back on the pedals and riding around in circles again.

"I love it," Francie replied, remembering the rainbow on the cave wall behind the waterfall. She moved her hand and watched as the prism cast rainbows against the wall of the house. She watched for a moment, and then realized with a stab of panic that she had nothing to give Ronan in return. She put the prism in her pocket and tried to think of anything she might have inside—maybe one of her books? Some of the herbs she had dried with her grandmother? But nothing she owned would make any sense to give to Ronan. Then she thought of the perfect gift.

"I have an idea of what to do," she said. "We don't need our bikes so you can leave yours here."

"What is it?"

"It's a secret," Francie responded.

"Just so that it doesn't involve breaking my other arm," Ronan joked.

"Well, I can't promise anything, but I think you should be okay." They left their bikes in the driveway and she led him through the garden and down the path into the woods.

When they came to the creek, Ronan told her that he still couldn't swim with his cast on.

"Don't worry," she replied. "We're just going to sit down there. I want to show you something."

They each sat on a rock in the sun and Francie closed her eyes. She tried to remember the song her grandmother had sung that day, weaving her own music in with the songs of the birds. She couldn't remember, but instead began to hum her own tune. She opened her eyes after a minute and looked up to see dozens of birds flying over their heads. They danced above and around them, in yellows and golds, bright greens and silvery blues. Ronan laughed as a yellow warbler landed on his arm and began to sing his own sweet-sweet-sweet song.

"It's kind of like a prism made of birds," Ronan said, as they looked up at all the colors swirling above them.

When Francie stopped humming, the birds flew away. She and

Ronan sat on the rocks for a while and let the cool water run over their feet.

"It's going to be kind of boring around here with you gone," Ronan said after a while.

"Yeah, I'm going to miss it here," she replied.

"You're really coming back next summer though?"

"I promise," Francie said.

They stayed until their feet began to ache from the cold creek water and then slowly made their way back to the garden.

"I guess I have someone else to send postcards to now," Francie said as they hugged goodbye. She watched as Ronan road his bike out of the driveway and down the road.

Chapter 30

Sylvie and Francie were both quiet on the drive to the airport. Francie would meet her mother at the gate and then an hour later the two of them would take a plane back to Los Angeles together. When they waited at the gate for her mother to arrive, Sylvie grabbed Francie's hand once and gave it a quick squeeze.

As usual, walking from the plane, Francie's mom stood out in the sea of people, wearing oversized black sunglasses and a tight pink sweater. When she saw Francie and Sylvie, she smiled and shrieked.

"Francie!" Her mother ran over and wrapped her arms around her.

"Hi Mom," Francie said, breathing in the familiar smell of her mom's perfume.

"Look at you!" her mother exclaimed, holding Francie at arm's length to look her over. "Wow, you've changed!"

Francie was startled. She had changed. She could ride a bike and hike a steep mountain; she had stood behind a waterfall and slept next a mountain lion; and she had learned to see the world in a whole new and magical way. She would never again look in the mirror and confuse herself with two dots and a line. She just hadn't realized it was so obvious from the outside.

"It's your hair," her mother was saying, nodding. "It's not frizzy anymore. You have beautiful curls!" She turned to Sylvie. "All these years of hundreds of products and apparently it just took some dry mountain air to get rid of that frizz."

Francie took a deep breath. "Thanks, Mom," she said and gave her a hug back.

- - -

Francie pressed her nose against the window as the plane began to wheel around for take off. The white and gray mountains stood starkly against a bright blue sky. Had she even noticed the view when she first arrived? It all looked so immense. She was comforted by the thought that somewhere in that range of mountains, she could picture a dusty little mountain town where Ronan rode his bike along a dirt road, her grandmother and Augustus shared a cup of tea and a mountain lion and her cub slept soundly together in their cave. She was glad that it was there and that she could picture it so vividly. An ache filled her heart, but it was mixed with hope. She would be back.

Acknowledgements

A year ago, my writing group, Sarah Peruzzi and Tara Schwarzbach, and Nanowrimo.org asked me the question: Can you write a novel in one month? The answer was no, but out of that first attempt, *Francie's Fortune* was born. Thank you for asking the question.

Thank you to my dad and my sister and to all of my friends who read the early drafts of my book and offered encouragement and support. And to Matt Lewis and Jerry Tuccille, I truly appreciate all of your help and insight on the industry.

A special thank you to my mom, who not only encouraged me from the beginning, but who designed the cover of this book.

To Blue Mustang Press, a heartfelt thanks for publishing *Francie's Fortune*.

And of course, to Toby, thank you for everything.